Wrath of the Falcon

Books by RV Hodge

Kingdom of the Falcon Series

Blood Trail of the Falcon
Ascent of the Falcon
Gepetka, Prince of Gypsies
Wrath of the Falcon

Children's Books

The Adventures of Boathouse Mouse

Book 1: A New Adventure, A New Name
Book 2: The Cat and the River Thames

Kingdom of the Falcon
Book IV

Wrath of the Falcon

by R V Hodge

Wrath of the Falcon   by RV Hodge

Copyright © 2016 RV Hodge

Printed in the United States of America

2016

ISBN 978-0-9975537-1-0

Dedicated to Josiah on his graduation from college.

May your arrows always fly true
May your fire always spin safely
May your shows always garner an audience
And may your music uplift people all over the world.

Love, Dad

Table of Contents

Pronunciation Guide

Gepetka	zheh-PET-kah
Lohman	LOW-mun
PenNel	PEN–NEL
Rhenska	REN-skah
Yomahito	YOH-mah-HEE-toh

Cousins

The hinges groaned slightly as the fourteen-year-old princess opened the old mahogany box with clandestine stealth. She carefully lifted several bundles out of the box until the flicker of candlelight fell on a note written in a different hand.

"This one," Princess Katrina whispered as she pulled the note out of the box.

Marisa stared intently as the light danced in her dark eyes. "Read it," Marisa urged in a whisper.

Katrina began, "It's addressed to Zeto. He's our great-great-grandfather. It's from his mother."

"Just read it," Marisa practically begged her cousin. Katrina read:

Dear Son, It is with deep sorrow that I recognize this place in which our people have chosen to gather. For though fifty years have passed since that dreadful day, I can still see it as if it was today. Our ancestors inhabited this valley for many generations. When I was a youth, a war raged through, and the citadel, of which my father was the last guardian steward, became a refuge for dozens of our villagers. When the battle came too near the citadel, my father rang the sacred bell. I can still hear its voice mingled with the weeping of mothers crouched with their children.

The promised reply from the neighboring king never came. In retrospect, I suspect he had already fallen.

The raiders partially broke the massive door enough to crawl in, and I cannot bring myself

"What do you think of that?" Katrina whispered.

"I've heard the riddle of the bell before, but never this part of the story," Marisa whispered back.

"That's because it was a deep secret. But with this, now we're going to find the citadel!" Katrina exclaimed.

"We don't even know if it's real," Marisa retorted skeptically, trying not to get swept along in her cousin's enthusiasm.

"It's real, all right. This note was from one of my ancestors," Katrina explained, as if that made it all make sense.

Marisa looked blank. "Mine too."

"Right. Our grandfather's grandfather found it. We're going to find it. Then we'll be famous, and maybe we'll even find treasure. Then we'll be rich too!" Katrina elaborated.

Marisa gave Katrina a funny look. "You're already rich. In case you forgot, you're the princess."

"Oh, don't do that! You're going to ruin the adventure," Katrina bemoaned.

"I don't see how you're going to have any adventure with your father's royal guard marching circles around you every minute of the day," Marisa challenged as she made a march pantomime with her fingers.

Katrina pulled herself close to Marisa and, after a theatrical look around to verify they were alone, whispered, "I've got it all planned out. When the boys go hunting, we'll slip past the guards in boys' clothing."

"Which boys are going hunting?" Marisa asked suspiciously.

"Samuel is taking my brother and your brother early the first morning," was Katrina's reply.

"My brother? Levi?" Marisa smirked.

"Yes, of course," Katrina replied tersely. "He's not so much the buffoon as everyone makes out!"

A light tap on the door as it swung open alerted the girls. They dove under their bedcovers, forgetting to put out the candles.

The maid smiled as she attempted to scold, "My Grace, you girls need your rest for the journey tomorrow."

The woman, whom the girls viewed as ancient, put out the candles as Katrina protested, "But, Miss Gretta, we can sleep in the carriage. The travel is insufferably boring."

"No carriage this time, M' Lady," the maid replied. "His Majesty's ordered horses for the two of you. You're to ride the whole way. He says it's too pretentious to show up to a Gypsy Jamboree in a royal coach."

A Fool and His Money

The villagers watched with baited anticipation as the Gypsy entertainer spun a large knife into the air. He had made the outrageous claim that he would make an apple and a ball disappear in a shower of fire and smoke. The audience had been skeptical, but he cajoled them until a man gave in and tossed a coin into his hat. That was the seed money the Gypsy knew would be necessary to get the rest to pay something after the show. The Gypsy had plied his tricks in villages all over Europe, and he knew the ropes of his trade.

With the large knife spinning nicely, the Gypsy added an apple and a cloth-wrapped ball to the juggling stream. As he did so, he rotated his show slightly to be done directly over his torch. The silent faces flickering in the yellow firelight showed their anticipation despite their earlier skepticism.

Once the eclectic items were spinning smoothly above the torch, the Gypsy began his monologue. "It is well known to the primitive tribal people in the darkest jungles of Africa that fire ghosts love apples above all else. Those hungry flames from the netherworld arrive and vanish without warning. But they always take an apple with them. So be very wary when you have an apple as close to the fire as I have this one, because you ..."

His words never finished. With precision timing borne of long practice, he caught the knife and nicked the thin fabric of the ball. Black powder granules showered out of the ball onto the torch. The ensuing yellow flash erupted up from the fire, seemingly of its own will. When the audience jumped with surprise, the Gypsy deftly flicked the apple to a grubby beggar at the edge of the crowd. The hungry pauper caught it greedily and slipped into the shadows to wolf down his prize.

The game of illusion was successful, and the audience was convinced they had observed magic firsthand. The cheers were encouraging to the Gypsy, but the coins being tossed into his hat were the reward he was after.

Levi preferred to use his hat for the collection rather than a bowl, for two reasons. The first was that he could not stand the pressure of hearing coins rattle into a dish and not knowing the amount. The second reason was a bit more practical. Levi the Entertainer did not want it to ever sound like he had made enough money. It was manipulative, he knew, but it was amazingly effective.

As he counted the money from that performance, Levi was satisfied that he had plenty to make it to the Gypsy Jamboree without any further interruptions. That night, he meticulously ladled a small measure of the fire granules into thin linen bags. They were each marked with a colored ribbon that corresponded to the color of fire that would flash out when they were ignited. After carefully hefting each one to determine equality, he stitched them tightly to create his juggling fire balls.

When he was satisfied with the way each ball came to hand, he carefully loaded them by the dozen into carry sacks. Those he stashed in inner pockets of each of his three cloaks.

Levi had strategically planned his shows for the Gypsy Jamboree to be progressively more impressive each night. His final performance would include many fire balls in the burn pit and, he was certain, would win him a chance to become a court jester in the kingdom.

With the much anticipated opportunity to dazzle the royal family, Levi left nothing to chance, hence the careful preparation for his upcoming shows. The following morning, Levi set out for the Jamboree. His heart was as free as a bird.

The Union of Evil

At the knock on the tavern door, the small port window was snatched open. The doorman looked hard for a moment, then slammed the small hatch closed. He turned and called to the tavern keeper, "It's Jarell."

The tavern, a well-known haunt of outlaws, was at the northern edge of the Kingdom of the Falcon. The keeper was a fat man with thinning, greasy, gray hair that was held in a sloppy ponytail. A perpetual drool line of tobacco stained the right side of his chin and traced its way down to the apron he wore. The apron appeared to have never been washed, and his establishment reflected the same level of cleanliness.

The fetid man made plenty of money operating a safe house for villains. He took a sizable cut from the tawdry women that worked his customers, and it was rumored that the little man was paid equally well to keep secrets as he was paid to sell them. In all, the shrewd little man had created the perfect environment for the nurturing of villainy at any level. By every measure of morality, it was a den of iniquity.

The tavern keeper glanced around the busy room to assess the crowd. Seeing no one he knew to be at odds with the notorious outlaw, he called back, "No bloodshed inside the house!"

The bouncer relayed the message, and the muffled reply sounded like assent. When the door was opened, Jarell entered, and the noise in the room dampened appreciably. In the momentary lull, a derisive voice called out, "Well, if it ain't Captain Jarell," mocking the title the infamous outlaw demanded his gang members use to address him. The tavern keeper sent a ferocious glance at the man who had called out the insult, and the room was subdued again.

Jarell scanned the room, and it was immediately obvious that he was looking for someone in particular. Before he could ask, the husky voice of a woman addressed him from behind. "Darling, I've been fending off these cretins all afternoon while waiting for you."

The outlaw whirled to see her, and was met with a warm embrace and a feigned kiss on the ear. The woman whispered, "Get us a room."

With the woman indiscreetly touching him, Jarell tossed a coin to the tavern keeper and ordered, "We need a room." The disconcerted look on his face reflected the paradox in Jarell's mind.

The keeper looked at the coin and nodded toward a back hallway, "First door on the right."

The woman resisted his movement when Jarell began to head toward the hall. "We need more privacy than that," she practically purred.

The keeper held out his hand, and Jarell grudgingly tossed him another coin. Again the head nodded and the keeper grunted, "Last room on the right."

Once the two were behind the rickety door of the room, Jarell hissed, "That's a pretty way to be discreet!"

"Hrmph. Every one of those pigs out there thinks they know what's happening in here. Now, what is this big deal you have going down?" she retorted coldly.

Their mutual disdain had kept them from working the same territory, but Jarell had put that aside, knowing the woman had a powerful gang. "I'm going to kidnap the prince for a ransom," Jarell answered briskly.

With arms crossed, the woman fixed her icy stare on him for a long moment. Finally she said, "I'm listening."

"I have an insider in the castle who tells me the prince is headed to a Gypsy gathering in the hill country around the solstice," Jarell replied. "There will only be a small caravan and a few royal guards accompanying him. I'm going to ambush them as they exit the river crossing, but I need more men. And this ain't the time to be breaking in green recruits. So I thought we could go in, even shares for everyone, and double for you and me."

"A prince's weight in gold," she mused aloud. It was obvious that greed had piqued her interest. "How heavy is the kid?"

"I don't know for sure. They say he's about the size of a medium man," Jarell replied, thinking of how much gold that would be.

"So, what do we do?" Her question signaled assent to the deal.

"I got it all planned out. The only thing is, there are two river crossings. And nobody is telling which route they're going. So I'll know when they take the fork in the road and we'll have a day to get set. If you wait at the village of Claystown, I'll send a messenger with a note. Black dot on the right side, we meet at the Old Miller's Ford. Black dot on the left side, we meet at Market Road Ford." Jarell seemed triumphant in his thorough planning.

The woman pondered a long moment before she asked, "How many men do you have?"

"Twenty," he lied by one.

"I'm bringing thirty and the ability to write," she replied, "I get three shares."

Jarell was agitated at being trivialized. "I'm the mastermind and I have the insider who can identify the prince! I get three shares!" he snapped back.

"We both get three shares then," she agreed.

He was annoyed, but his greed won the internal fight, and he consented. As a last attempt to establish dominance in the new arrangement, Jarell mentioned, "You aren't known around these parts. So, just follow my lead."

She gave him a condescending smirk and simply replied, "I will be."

"Split an arrow!" one of the Gypsy children cried out excitedly. The sentiment spread instantly and, in two heartbeats, all the children began the chant, "Split an arrow! Split an arrow! Split an arrow!"

The woodsman waved his hands to quiet his crowd of spectators. It had been a few years since Samuel had made the annual gathering of his people. He was a Gypsy of the band and lineage of Gepetka. He was also a woodsman in the Kingdom of the Falcon, and a member of the Archers.

The Archers had been created by Lord William as an elite level of kingdom guard within the franchise of woodsmen. They served with the ranks of the gamekeepers, but had the extended duty as patrols within the wild lands of the kingdom. Many fugitive criminals had been apprehended or run out of the kingdom by Lord William's ever-vigilant Archers. They were few in number, but strong in skill, stealth, and surprise, and Samuel was proud to be counted in their numbers.

However, even as an elite Archer, Samuel did not have the same confidence that William had about splitting arrows at will. Still, he was tempted to give it a try. When his gesturing finally calmed the excited mob of children, Samuel was about to capitulate, but before he could speak, the drum of wing beats was heard. Quite by chance, a grey partridge landed on an old stump in the target range.

Inspiration can be the fine line separating glory from folly. Samuel's single fluid motion took an arrow from his quiver and sent it to the partridge even as the bird's feet alighted on the stump. In the eyes of the Gypsy children, it was as if he had somehow summoned the bird to land where he knew the arrow would strike. "Samuel commands the forest animals!" became the next great subject of their excited cheers.

In the frenzy of activity that took place when the children sprinted to retrieve the arrow and the welcomed addition to their feast, Samuel tried to explain how splitting arrows was wasteful. But, for the greatest part, his effort was in vain. And thus it often goes, that the true insights of an accomplished man are overlooked, and he gets branded with an imaginary persona.

As the children rushed into the gathering Gypsy camp to spread the news, the Gypsy Queen appeared, seemingly from thin air. She mused, "The children idolize you, Samuel. They see in you what is not realistic because they believe it is possible. Do not fret over what you cannot change, only burden yourself with those things within your control."

With a parting smile, she patted his elbow. He pondered her words as he watched the frail old woman wander back into the camp. She was on a mission, he presumed, to startle someone else.

Levi came to Samuel before anyone else came back to the archery field. "I've been practicing all year." He nodded toward his bow. "I may not be able to arrow more boars than you and Lohman, but I'll not be missing any shots this year."

Samuel was amused at his cousin's declaration of confidence. He knew Levi was reassuring himself as much as anything else. He and Lohman could finish any boar that Levi could wound. "Stick three into the second target quickly!" Samuel abruptly ordered.

Levi immediately drew and shot the arrows in quick succession. He had anticipated that kind of command based on the training he had received from Samuel in the prior years. The shots were all on target and, while it was by no means spectacular, Samuel praised his cousin, "Well, well, you will not starve with that kind of shooting!"

Levi was elated. However, not wanting to risk being the ruin of their planned hunt, he continued to practice for the next two hours. After gathering his arrows from the targets the final time, Levi turned and discovered that Prince Lohman had been watching him. Lohman called out, "Well done, Cousin. Samuel said you were shooting very well. I may leave my bow in camp tomorrow. You'll probably arrow all the boars before I could even nock an arrow."

Levi knew that Lohman was exaggerating. Since his youth, the prince had been trained in all disciplines of warfare. Levi suspected Lohman could probably shoot nearly as well as Samuel. But Levi had been the lifelong brunt of jests, and it was nice to hear his cousins recognize he had improved to some degree of proficiency. For the first time in his life, he was really looking forward to the next day's hunt. He mused to himself, *The Jamboree this year will be remembered.*

The Brewing Storm

She was a loathsome woman on the rare occasion when she was in a good mood. The rest of the time, she was completely incorrigible. The smoky room was deathly silent as she stared across the rim of her mug at the burly youth who had just delivered the message.

The messenger stood trembling before the notorious outlaw. He had been flippant, even cocky, about his task, until he saw the look in her eyes. He had the sudden notion that the rumors about the woman were true. For a fleeting second, he considered drawing his dagger and attacking her. His mind raced through all he knew about how to dispatch a witch, and he came up blank. In the close presence of the thirty or so thugs that made up her gang, he decided to try tact. "I could take a reply to Jarell and this, this misunderstanding could be cleared up. And there's maybe still time to find, … you know …" An involuntary tear beaded in the corner of the terrified lad's eye as he lowered his voice to a quavering whisper, "… the prince."

"So, what is your name, dear?" the woman asked in a disarmingly casual tone.

The stunned youth stammered, "P-Peter."

She stood and calmly asked the lad, "Peter, darling, do you know this man?" She was pointing at the wide-eyed innkeeper. The messenger shook his head in the negative. "How about his lovely daughter?" She indicated a homely girl of about twelve years. The innkeeper stepped in front of his daughter. Again the messenger shook his head.

The woman lifted her staff. It was of a peculiar design, made in equal parts of wood and iron. She pointed the staff at the innkeeper and simply stated, "Remember this, Peter," as she gently squeezed a lever. Yellow flame erupted from the staff. The room resounded in a deafening roar as the man was launched backward over his daughter. The thick smell of brimstone left by the flame confirmed in the young man's mind that this woman was indeed a witch. Her magical power evident, Peter all but fainted. She gently brushed a stream of tears from his face and calmly said, "Poor thing. Dry his tears, Lou."

Rough hands grabbed the hapless youth, and his face was forced against the hot stones of the hearth. The smell of burning flesh was accompanied by his screams of pain. Then he was yanked to face the woman again. She crooned, "Tell Jarell, when Rhenska receives his message with a dot on the right side of a parchment, his idiot messenger really should open it the correct direction. And if he doesn't want to be partners in this business venture, I'll be happy to remove him."

She patted the boy's face on the non-burned side and gently turned his chin to see the lifeless form of the innkeeper. The hysterical girl was futilely trying to staunch the gaping hole in her father's chest. When the lad was able to pry his eyes from the morbid scene, Rhenska met his befuddled gaze. She put her face very close to the lad's ear and whispered, "Remind Jarell we'll see him by sunset tomorrow. And, Peter, give him this for me." Whereupon she kissed the lad's cheek.

The messenger stared in hopeless confusion at the woman as she calmly ordered, "Well, let him go to his errand."

The last thing the Peter heard as he exited the inn was Rhenska's voice calmly ordering, "Burn this place. It's a mess."

*   *   *   *   *

A bleary-eyed man, in the back of the room, sat rooted in abject horror as the scene unfolded before him. He had been ignored. He had been ignored for over a decade, since no one takes the village drunk seriously. The man had been too terrified to even fidget. However, when the gang raked coals from the fireplace onto the inn floorboards, the rapidly sobering drunkard dropped to his hands and knees below the table. The gang trampled out the door, and the building rapidly filled with flames. Hurriedly, the drunk crawled toward the back door. He noticed the traumatized girl sobbing across the body of her father and, though he was by no means a hero, he crawled to the girl and grabbed her arm. Half dragging, half pleading, he managed to get the girl out of the burning building and hidden behind a nearby shed.

*   *   *   *   *

At the cave where Jarell had set up his headquarters, there was a great ruckus as Peter, the young messenger, forced his way past the guard. "You gotta' halt and declare yourself, boy! Or you'll get a pike in the liver!" the guard shouted as Peter rushed in, shrieking, to report to Jarell.

"She's a witch! It's true!" Peter nearly cried as he grabbed Jarell's tunic. "Captain Jarell, she can speak fire and death from her staff! Don't let her join us!"

The lad broke down into sobs as he poured out the story of the trauma he had witnessed. The gang leader was irritated by the boy's wanton fear, but Jarell had harbored some of those same fears himself. The burned face was a gristly reminder that Rhenska would be a brutal adversary. But the one thing Jarell already knew was that Rhenska had an arquebus. He also understood its limitations.

Jarell pondered the imbalance of power that he was flirting with. Rhenska had thirty men to his twenty. But they would need the force of numbers to handle the royal guard. He also knew her favored tactic was hand-to-hand combat. Jarell assessed his gang with a quick glance. *Five bowmen*, he pondered smugly to himself, *and one of them is Francis ... The Bowman. That is how I balance the power, you old witch.*

Jarell let his mind jump ahead in the scenario of his plan. He visualized their ultimate success, and an arrow flying from Francis's bow into Rhenska's heart. His muse was interrupted by Peter's pleading.

"Captain, she's not even human … she's a witch from the netherworld! I don't think she has a heart," the lad babbled through shameless tears.

Jarell was yanked back to the immediate situation. "Did anyone say anything about her heart?" Jarell snapped ferociously, fearing he had spoken his secret thoughts aloud.

Peter was startled out of his paroxysm by Jarell's forceful words. "Um, no sir, Captain," he replied timidly.

"Get ahold of yourself, boy! I'll send you back to that dirt farm in a heartbeat if you blubber like a little girl ever again! You're seventeen years old and bigger than most men! Act like it!" Jarell's hand was on the hilt of his sword as he chided the big youth.

Peter wisely shut his mouth and slipped into a dark corner of the cave. As he lay there, he thought about the relentless plight of his uncle's farm. The work was never finished and there was never any hope of more than the next day's food. He wondered if his uncle would let him return. With fitful thoughts, the lad fell asleep.

The Jamboree Begins

Merriment was abundant at the Gypsy Jamboree. In addition to the usual excitement, the arrival of Crown Prince Lohman and Princess Katrina on the eve of the first day had made everything more intense. To their delight, the royal youths were whisked into the jubilation and dragged from one experience to the next. The promised visit by the king and queen on the last days of the Jamboree further compounded the exuberance.

The royal guard was not nearly so delighted, as a Gypsy Jamboree is the exact opposite of orderly security. But they adapted as best they could to the turbulent activity. The whole event was an exercise in frustration for the royal guard, but that was all part of their duty in protecting the prince and princess.

The prince, at age fifteen, did not present so much of a concern to the royal guard. He was levelheaded, and was almost always in the presence of Samuel. Samuel's position as an Archer in Lord William's service allowed him into the inner circle of trusted guardians. And there was an added benefit that he was of some kin to the queen, and thus the prince. Samuel's expertise with a bow was well known, and he was in all considerations an unofficial personal bodyguard to the prince.

The princess was a different story altogether. At the age of fourteen, her whimsical pursuits were an unpredictable mixture of childishly innocent delights and profoundly imaginative explorations. She routinely slipped through the crowds in a way that impeded the progress of her assigned guards. Indeed, she viewed the practice of evading her own protectors as sporting. In the mind of Princess Katrina, it was all in great fun. In the mind of Captain Cornelius, it was flabbergasting.

*   *   *   *   *

The spontaneous festivities of the day had been embellished to entertain the royal heirs. Everyone wanted a turn to show their craft to their honored guests, so it was later than usual before Levi got his moment of glory.

After everyone had eaten and the storytelling had begun in earnest, Levi pulled out his first show. When it was known that his performance would include a razor-sharp knife and a torch, there were many hoots and jests made about his notorious ability to attract trouble. When he began to toss the torch into the air, the jokes doubled. When he added the knife and an apple to the items in the air, everyone became very silent. For though they had made jokes, no one wished him any ill.

To the astonishment of the Gypsies and royal visitors alike, Levi juggled the eclectic items expertly. To further compound their amazement, he kept up a steady monologue. "So, I saw this farmer, who didn't look particularly bright, trying to harness a cur dog and a pig to his plow. Before I had a chance to suggest it was a bad idea, that pig nipped at the dog and the fight began. Round and round they went, squealing and snarling, both animals trying to get at the other, but tangling the lines all around that old man! It didn't take but a minute before that fellow was head down, tied up in his own harnesses, and the animals had chewed out free, and were tearing up the garden!

"While he's hanging there calling for help, his old lady comes out with a broom, yelling and fussing at the pig and the dog, but since she can't catch up to the animals, she gives the old man a beating while he's hanging there!"

Once he had his audience in stitches, Levi flicked the knife through the apple and stuck it into the torch handle. With a deft slap as he caught the torch, the apple was severed neatly, and the halves fell to the laps of the prince and princess. That they each caught their half in the air was testimony that both royal heirs had inherited the gifted vision from their father.

The audience was raucously appreciative, and even the royal guards were momentarily caught up in the applause. But a sudden sensation set Captain Cornelius on edge. He loosed his sword in its scabbard as he called his guards to order. Each man returned dutifully to his assigned post and instinctively loosened his sword as the captain had done. Knowing the captain had sensed something amiss, the guards stared intently into the dark forest outside the camp.

Captain Cornelius vigilantly spent most of the night slipping quietly from one post to the next. By daybreak, he was slightly irked that his sensation had not been rewarded with anything tangible.

Honor Among Thieves

The messenger came panting into the camp. He had run stumbling through the moonlit night to bring the news. "Captain Jarell," the young man panted, "Captain Jarell! They got a lot of them royal guards in the Gypsy camp. I counted twenty-one, and one commander that kept roaming around and looking into the woods right at me. I think he can see in the dark."

The man stopped his report abruptly when he saw the woman with his leader. His eyes shifted uncertainly back and forth between the two gang leaders, for when he had left the camp to spy on the Gypsies, she and her gang had not been there. There had even been talk of a war between the two gangs after the botched message about the river crossing location of the prince's party. Suspicion runs deep among thieves and murderers. At the commotion, the rest of both gangs gathered around.

"Spill it out, Franklin," Jarell demanded.

"In front of her, Captain?" Franklin asked hesitantly.

"We have come to an amicable arrangement. Get on with your report!" Jarell snapped. He looked anything but amicable.

"The prince is in the camp, for sure. I saw 'im. The guards follow 'im around everywhere. The king's party ain't showed yet." The man paused as if trying to think of a good spin on the next news. "And … and they got a woodsman too," Franklin said with a degree of despair in his voice.

Jarell's eyes widened a bit, but before he could ask anything, Rhenska cut in incredulously, "A game warden? Your goons are afraid of a game warden?"

"Not Lord Archer, right?" Jarell asked with an unusual degree of calmness. "He's not supposed to be there 'til the fourth day."

"Not him. I don't know who this one is, but he's got marked arrows," Franklin replied.

"You boys have to tell me why we are worrying over a woodsman. This is ridiculous." Rhenska nearly raised her voice.

Jarell paced around for a few minutes before he asked, "Do you think they suspect anything?"

"I don't think so, sir, but we better make a move soon, before the king gets there," Franklin answered.

Rhenska was irritated at being excluded from the planning. "I am providing the greater force, so we'll be doing things my way."

"I have the insider, and I can identify the prince!" Jarell snapped. "I'll be making the orders!"

"I have an arquebus," she all but crooned as she lowered the barrel toward Jarell. "In one second, I can have the insider and this dolt to identify the prince. That makes me the leader."

Jarell pushed the weapon away from himself and snarled, "I've got a bowman who has his eye on your every move! If you so much as point that thing in my direction again, he'll put an arrow between your shoulder blades in a heartbeat! And just in case you get some fool notion, my insider is mute and I'm the only one who can communicate with him!"

Rhenska's composure slipped up a bit as she snapped, "We're using a deaf spy to get information from the palace?"

"He's not deaf, you ...! He's not deaf. Just mute," Jarell growled.

There was a sullen silence for a few minutes. Rhenska felt outmaneuvered, which made her internally furious, but her demeanor became more passive when she was angry. Finally Jarell made the command, "We'll overrun the camp tomorrow night when they are having their nightly binge. There'll be no grabbing of women or anything else, 'cause we're gonna need every blade at work on those guards! They've only got twenty-three, counting the woodsman, and we got almost fifty. And we got surprise on our side. And you," he pointed at Rhenska, "are going to deal with the woodsman."

Guessing that the men had been in isolation for a long time, Rhenska seamlessly transitioned to feminine charm. She casually placed her hand on Franklin's chest. Ever so gently she stroked up to his shoulder as she gave a little pout. "What is it about this woodsman that makes even you worried?"

She was too old for that kind of play. But her tactic paid off. "Well, um, ma'am, the woodsmen are known to dabble in the arts. Or rumored to anyway. The ones with marked arrows, they're very … dangerous," Franklin stammered as his face reddened.

It was Jarell's turn to be outmaneuvered. He was agitated by how easily she had bypassed his authority with her feigned charm. But, taking a cue from her style, he calmly suggested, "Unless you're afraid your magic arquebus is not a match for his abilities …"

To the astonishment of all present, she sauntered close to Jarell and whispered, "I'm not afraid … ever." Then, as if condemning him, she kissed his cheek.

Struggling to regain his composure, Jarell added, "We got to keep that kid in good shape, so don't be ruffin' him up! We'll truss him up in the cave and, well, then we split up the gold!" A thought occurred to Jarell at that moment. "Franklin. 'Bout how much you think the kid weighs?"

"I don't know about that, Captain. Not too good at weights. He's maybe about Matson's size," Franklin guessed.

Matson looked up from the chunk of bread he was gnawing. Around a mouthful he managed, "Ten stone weight. Least, when I was in the games, it was."

Avarice went suddenly thick in the hearts of all those present. Franklin stated what everyone else was thinking: "That's a lot of gold."

Boar Hunting

At the daybreak guard change, when it was time for the posts to report, Captain Cornelius' mood seemed pensive. In stark contrast, shafts of sunlight filtered through the treetops, illuminating the fog and smoke with a cheerful glow. Seeming older than his years, the captain called his men to order for reports. He began with, "Gentlemen, if last night was a false alarm, I'll be beaten. It is our duty to protect the heirs to the crown with all due diligence and even outright suspicion."

He paused for a moment to collect his thoughts, then continued. "There was something afoul out there. I sensed it. I smelled it. I don't know how I know, but something was out there last night. We mustn't let our guard relax."

No one questioned the captain's assessment. He was notorious for his ability to sense trouble in advance, although some of the men wondered if the strange surroundings and Gypsy mystique had caused him to overreact. They did not have much time to entertain that idea, as the captain called out for the watch reports.

There were several routine reports. Then one which included an intoxicated elderly widow woman who repeatedly flirted with one of the guards. Her antics were recounted and elicited a hardy round of laughter at the guard's expense. Then came a report that all was routine, including the prince and the juggler leaving the camp an hour before daybreak as planned for their boar hunting expedition.

Cornelius looked up sharply and asked, "Was not Samuel the Woodsman with them?"

The sergeant that had made the report turned a deep red as he responded, "The prince whispered that Samuel was out of the camp awaiting them. I did question him. Those woodsmen are ... are an independent lot, sir."

"Very well," Cornelius grumbled in a tone that meant the opposite.

"Sir." Another guard stepped out of turn for his report.

Captain Cornelius was patient, thoughtful, and considerate. He was also orderly. He eyed the guard just long enough to recognize the man had something urgent to add. "Yes?" he asked tersely.

"Sir, the three hunters exited the camp via my post at two hours before daybreak. I could clearly make out each of their crests on their cloaks. Also, Samuel is known to me personally and I recognized his voice."

There was a long silence as the captain looked back and forth between the two guards with conflicting reports. The tension was tangible, and it showed up on the furrowed brow of the captain. He queried, "Did anyone observe the prince and ... what's that juggler's name?

"Levi, sir."

"Did anyone observe the prince and Levi reenter the camp between two hours and one hour prior to dawn?" The captain chose his words with care.

Each of the guards shifted uncomfortably as the captain's gaze rested on them. "Is it possible that they did so in complete secrecy?" he asked with a mixture of disdain and agitation. "I would like to believe that even Samuel the Woodsman would have to work diligently to slip past my elite guard in the night watch. I cannot, under any circumstance, believe the prince and that noisy Gypsy could possibly do so."

There was an awkward pause of several minutes before Captain Cornelius stated, "If anyone has a failure of diligence to confess, it will go much better for you now than when the prince returns and I learn the whole truth."

The frustration was evident on the captain's face as he looked inquisitively at each of the guards that had been on post during the time in question. Each responded with a negative head shake to indicate he had nothing to confess. "So be it," Cornelius muttered in disappointment.

A general feeling of disunity hovered over the royal guard as the captain read off the duty assignments for the day. As the men were dispersing to their assigned places, Gretta, the maid to the princess, hurried up to the captain.

"Captain, sir?" Gretta asked with a nervous voice. "Have you seen My Lady, the princess, this morning?"

"You've lost the princess?" He responded with the tone of voice that surfaces when everything else is going wrong.

"They seem to have slipped out early, sir. And I can't find them anywhere." Gretta was nearly in tears.

"They?" Cornelius asked.

"Princess Katrina and Marisa, her cousin ... the Gypsy girl," she replied uncomfortably.

The captain whistled a short signal and, turning back to Gretta, asked, "What was the princess wearing?"

As the guard hastily assembled in report formation, Gretta shuffled her feet and stammered incomprehensibly through piteous sniffles.

Captain Cornelius never looked away from Gretta as he addressed his men. "The princess' maid seems to have lost track of the princess. She was accompanied by the Gypsy girl she has been running about with. Two girls can't have gotten themselves too far from their quarters, so we will fan out throughout the camp and locate them quickly." He paused to survey his men, then reiterated, "Good lady, what were they wearing?"

Gretta turned deep shades of red as if caught in some secret sin. "I'm not so certain, sir, but they didn't put on what I had laid out for them." She shuffled uncomfortably then blurted, "I'm afraid they've dressed themselves up like lads."

There was a protracted silence as the guard members observed the scene in confusion. It was obvious that Cornelius was baffled as well. Tentatively he asked, "Like lads?"

"Oh, sir, 'tis my business to keep Her Grace's things in order. I wasn't snooping, but I came across a cloak of the prince's and the Gypsy Levi's as well, all bundled up behind the bedding yesterday, then when the girls were missing and their clothes were not, I checked, and I think the princess and her cousin have dressed themselves up to look like their brothers!" Gretta's statement came flooding out in one long exclamation and was punctuated with a slight sob.

Captain Cornelius was by nature stoic and composed. However, when the realization of the situation dawned on his mind, his face turned a ghastly pale color. He looked at the sergeant and hoarsely stated, "The princess is out of the camp." He hesitated as his hand ran involuntarily through his hair. Then turning, he gazed into the forest as if expecting a sign. "The princess is … completely out of our protection," was all he could utter.

The captain paced slowly back and forth with his eyes cast down. It was apparent to the men he was whispering. No one could tell if he was making prayers or merely rambling to himself. When he snapped his head up, his men were startled, but expectant. "Do the Gypsies keep hounds?" he asked.

There was some curious and furtive glancing that took place. Finally, one of the men said, "I don't think so, sir. They seem to have an aversion to dogs in general."

Cornelius looked off into the woods again. His eyes searched back and forth as if he were trying to follow the princess with his mind. Rhetorically he muttered, "Could it be any worse?"

As if to ominously answer his question, there was a distant boom that re-echoed down the valley.

"You idiot! Don't shoot the prince!" Jarell nearly screamed in Rhenska's ear.

Rhenska leveled an icy stare into Jarell's eyes and hissed, "I put the prince to flight away from his bodyguard. And don't ever call me out again."

Her lie was convincing. She had indeed fired on the prince, but the accuracy of the primitive weapon and her personal ability limited its effectiveness to a short range. However, despite the bungling on her part, it had actually worked remarkably well. The shot from the arquebus had set the prince running in the opposite direction from the other two hunters. He was also running away from the Gypsy camp and the royal guards. Someone pointed to the other two, who were frantically racing up the trail that led to the Gypsy camp. "What about those two?"

Rhenska shouted in derision. "Your dreaded game warden has tucked tail and is running for all he's worth to get away from me. But the gold is running that way. Get him!"

As dozens of men raced off in pursuit of the prince, Jarell yelled out, "Bring him alive! He ain't worth nothin' dead!"

Jarell and Rhenska paced about the camp nervously. They openly detested each other, so naturally they avoided contact. The promise of tremendous riches was the only bond that kept them united in the odd partnership. Rhenska slipped into the cave to reload the arquebus in secret. She had kept the aggravatingly slow process hidden from her men. For their part, they had no idea it was not an endless supply of shots. She reveled in the fear she commanded. As she reloaded the weapon, Rhenska mused to herself that she would eventually end up with the entire ransom of gold. *Ah, patience*, she thought. *Every man that goes down to dust is another share in my hands.*

"Switch cloaks with me now," hissed Marisa.

The girls had almost walked directly into the camp full of criminals and, at the last minute, had dropped into the thick underbrush. They had actually seen the hunting party with the prince as they had fled in two directions, and Marisa had to clap her hand over Princess Katrina's mouth when Rhenska had fired a shot at the fleeing prince.

After the men in the camp had left, the girls had overheard the whole exchange. They had cautiously crept away from the camp and skirted a long way around before Marisa dared make a sound.

"Give me your cloak," she whispered again.

"Why?" Katrina's mind was far away, thinking of her brother being pursued.

"That is the prince's cloak. If they see us, they'll chase after me," Marisa argued. "You can sneak back to camp."

"Marisa, we have to find Lohman and see if he needs help," Katrina urged as they exchanged cloaks.

Marisa wanted to console Katrina, but she was filled with dread herself. "We need to get you back to the safety of your father's guards." Then grabbing the princess's hand, Marisa led the way, but they did not get far. Every direction the girls tried, they encountered small groups of the gang. The outlaws were noisy on the trails and worse in the thickets, which was the only reason the princess and Marisa were able to successfully avoid contact. But escape was thwarted at every turn.

The outlaws had become frustrated right away. None of them were particularly bright, and every forest sound set them off thrashing through the underbrush. Before long, they sorted into small groups and began crisscrossing the countryside. They also set up a watchman at all the major trail crossroads. Several of the men had signal whistles, so they were naturally posted as the watchmen.

Running back and forth, and even attempting a cross-country trek, the girls became exasperated by the persistent threat. After a couple of hours, Katrina began to slow down with fatigue. Marisa took Katrina close to a rock overhang near a stream. She whispered, "You must wait here. I'll run back to camp and get the guards. But you must stay hidden."

Katrina attempted to protest, "They will capture you! We need to stick together." But her soft life had not prepared her to run for her life through the forest.

"No. You're slowing me down. I'm going to go through the forest and draw them away from here. You just rest for a while," Marisa insisted. The disappointment was evident on Katrina's face, but she ultimately agreed.

When Marisa slipped away from the hiding place alone, she was able to elude the thugs for a good while. She realized when she was halfway back to the Gypsy camp that without Katrina, she might be able to make it the whole way without detection. The thought was appealing, but she knew if she did so, the gang would continue searching, which put Katrina at the greatest risk.

As Marisa got closer to the Gypsy camp, the number of brushes with the outlaws diminished. She could hear them off in the distance. There were occasional shouts, and the sound of a signal whistle a few times. She was on edge when she heard those sounds, but they had been happening all the while she and Katrina were hiding.

She had not seen anyone for a while when she came to the last creek crossing before the camp. It was a gently bubbling stream about a mile from the Gypsy camp, and the Gypsy children had typically made at least one group foray to it each Jamboree. It was a rite of passage, of sorts, for the children who became old enough to venture off into the woods. It was relatively safe under normal circumstances.

At that crossing, Marisa spotted one of the thugs on guard duty. He was leaning back against a boulder, fast asleep.

She could have slipped past him and made it to the camp, but she knew that would not protect the princess. Gently she crossed the shallow ford. When she was past the man a few yards, she threw a stone at the man. The hit was directly to his face, and the effect was immediate.

The man jumped to his feet, howling, as Marisa bolted down the trail. His shrill whistle followed quickly and others could be heard responding to the panicked signal.

Nearly twenty men pursued the Gypsy girl, whom they mistook to be the prince because of the cloak. But she was in superior physical shape from walking everywhere all her life. And she had the added incentive that she was scared for her life. The tired men never had a chance to catch her, but they chased her until they knew it was too late.

*　　*　　*　　*　　*

Katrina had stayed hidden long enough to doze off for a while. She had no idea what happened, but a signal whistle was sounded so near her that she jolted awake. With heart racing, she heard nearby shouts and curses as men trampled down a trail. Feeling like her hiding spot was compromised, she crept further up the stream. After a few minutes of sneaking slowly, her imagination got the better of her, and she began to run.

When she had run until her sides felt like they would burst, Katrina collapsed in some thick grass by the stream. She lay there gasping for a long time, and eventually faded off to sleep once again. As she slept, a suspicious sound crept into her subconsciousness. It was the kind of sound that is eerie because of what is missing rather than what is heard.

29

Her eyes opened abruptly as Katrina realized someone was intentionally being furtive with their movements. Unconsciously she held her breath while straining her eyes in the direction the stalker was coming from. Her mind raced, *Had someone seen her? Had the villains become that systematic?*

When the man was close enough that she could hear his breathing, she had the sudden realization that he had been running too. Ever so quietly, Katrina's hand closed around the hilt of her dagger. Gently, she lifted her head just enough to peek and saw a man peering down the trail. He had come from the opposite direction and was intently watching where he had come from.

A slight breeze moved the grass, and Katrina saw the crest on his cloak. "Lohman?" was all she could gasp.

Gypsy Chaos

A Gypsy Jamboree was long on excitement and short on organization. When a stress or trauma was added to it, the precarious order of things tended to degenerate quickly. So it was that when word swept through the camp that the princess was missing, chaos erupted. Not everyone was alarmed, which contributed to much of the confusion, as there were numerous animated debates over what should be done.

Captain Cornelius and his royal guard were at their wits' end. In attempting to track down people that the princess may have spoken to, then interview them to determine where the girls might have gone, they were more confused than ever.

The chaos within the camp continued for hours. Many people came to the captain with conflicting information, some of which was obviously fantasy. Captain Cornelius was trying to discern fact from fancy as an elderly woman was talking to him, when a cry rippled through the Gypsy camp.

The cry was raised a third time before everyone went quiet.

The first words Cornelius heard were, "Samuel and Levi have returned!" Then he heard, "Samuel and the prince have returned!"

Cornelius raced to the epicenter of the excitement and forced his way through the throng of Gypsies. "Samuel!" he called out, "Where are you? Where is the prince?"

The crowd shifted a bit, and suddenly Captain Cornelius was face-to-face with Prince Lohman wearing Levi's cloak.

"Your Highness!" Cornelius exclaimed, "I am so relieved you are safe!"

The ensuing confusion and chatter were overwhelming to Captain Cornelius, who finally snapped at Samuel, "Where can we go to get some privacy, and quiet, from these people?"

Samuel held up his arms and called out over the din, "Captain Cornelius requires a council with the elders immediately!"

Cornelius protested, "I just want to speak with you, the prince, and my men! In peace and quiet!"

Samuel shrugged as he responded, "These people are all family. Everyone is into everyone's business. The best way to get peace and quiet is an elder council. Besides that, you may get some wise advice from them."

Cornelius was thoroughly exasperated. "I don't really need their wisdom! I need peace, quiet, and facts!"

Samuel was tired, but persistent. "Sir, you can't have it both ways here. This is the best peace and quiet you can get. And ... you might be surprised at what these people know."

Cornelius capitulated grudgingly.

Council of the Hunter

Samuel told his story quickly to the captain and the royal guard. The Gypsy elders listened in. "We left camp two hours before dawn as planned and headed into Shady Valley in hopes of finding some boars. Near the place where the old city ruins are, going toward the old ferry crossing, we stumbled upon a large camp of men. It was slothful in every appearance and we deemed it to be the camp of rogues. So we took our leave of the area as quickly as possible, but someone spotted us and raised a cry. There must have been fifty men in that camp, and I clearly heard, 'The prince has come to us! Get him!'

"My blood curdled as the implications swept through my mind. The first impulse was to make a stand, but one woodsman, one prince, and ... and, well, Levi the Entertainer ... it seemed like a poor strategy. There was a pause when everyone in the camp just gawked at us, and Levi ..." Samuel had to pause because the emotion for his cousin came to his eyes for a moment.

Prince Lohman interjected, "Levi had given me his woolen cloak earlier, because I was cold in the morning mountain air. He was wearing mine with the royal crest. He was brilliant. He just whispered, 'Run!' Then, without an instant's hesitation, he ran in the opposite direction. He knew he would be the decoy and placed himself in mortal danger on my behalf."

"We seized the opportunity and ran back here," Samuel began.

The prince added, "I insisted we go to Levi's aid immediately."

"The prince's safety is of supreme concern and non-negotiable, regardless of the cost," Samuel retorted, half to the prince and half to the captain.

"You did right," Captain Cornelius affirmed. Prince Lohman looked annoyed by the judgment.

Samuel took a deep breath, then continued the story. "We had taken no more than fifty running paces when a thunderous roar shook us. It was one of the villainous rogues with an arquebus. He fired at Levi. I do not know if Levi was struck, but the entire camp charged after Levi, and they never gave us a second look as we raced back here to camp."

Prince Lohman sprang to his feet and demanded, "Captain Cornelius, I command you to devote every possible resource to find and, if he's alive, rescue Levi. His selfless action was nothing less than heroic!"

"No," the captain replied immediately.

The prince looked stricken.

Samuel offered, "Sir, I will go alone and recover Levi. This is my craft. Only you really need to take the prince and princess away from this place. They're in serious jeopardy as long as that gang is at large. Also, the king must be warned."

Samuel paused and looked around the camp, then added, "And it's not fair to the Gypsies. They should not be subjected to the dangers associated with politics that are not their concern."

Captain Cornelius stared at Samuel for a long moment, then asked, "So you have not heard about the princess?"

Samuel and the prince exchanged blank glances. Cornelius continued, "Her Grace has apparently slipped out of camp this morning. No one knows where she has gone, or why."

Samuel felt like he should say something, but his mind was stunned.

In the painful silence that accompanies the feeling of helplessness among powerful men, an aged Gypsy woman spoke up in a raspy voice. "Marisa and the princess have gone exploring for the ancient citadel." All eyes turned to the old woman. Slowly, deliberately, she responded to the question in their eyes. "We were all young once. That old legend can't seem to lie dormant in the presence of imaginative children. Besides, they asked aplenty of questions about it."

Cornelius was speechless for a moment, then he asked, "Where is this place?"

The old woman's face drew into a mournful look. She replied, "It is unknown … but believed to be in the vicinity of the old ferry crossing."

"Would that be the same …?" With his half-asked question directed at Samuel, the captain already knew the answer. Cornelius was stricken with fear deep in his heart, but his court manners returned, and he said to the Gypsy council, "I am deeply sorry that our business has put your people in the way of harm. I have my sworn duty to uphold to the last breath. Your people may wish to leave the region quickly, as this may escalate into a great deal of bloodshed."

The old woman looked at each of the elders present before she replied, "We will provide support for your soldiers, and messengers to the king, and any other assistance you may need. Remember, son, that princess is one of us. There are three of our people out there at this very moment."

Captain Cornelius was clearly out of options. With Samuel's and the prince's help, he drafted a note to be delivered to the king. A young Gypsy with a horse was chosen to deliver the note, and plans and maps were being crudely drawn in the dirt when a cry went up, "The princess is back!"

Levi jumped in shock when a girl's voice called out behind him.

"Lohman?"

Levi whirled around with speed which he did not know he possessed. His dagger had rather appeared in his hand of its own will as he faced the voice that called out behind him. He was nothing short of astonished.

"Levi? What are you doing wearing my brother's cloak?" Princess Katrina demanded with all authority.

Levi didn't blink, but retorted indignantly, "What are you doing wearing **my** cloak? You're wearing my clothes!"

Katrina looked at her garb and shrugged. "Your sister got us clothes so we could slip out of camp unnoticed and go exploring." Her reply was so casual, Levi wondered if such practices were commonplace amongst royal heirs.

"Lohman and I, er … the prince and I traded cloaks when it was cold this morning. This one isn't very warm." Levi felt suddenly self-conscious in the royal cloak.

They had a silent moment, then the princess, suddenly concerned, asked, "Were you harmed when that man fired that dreadful arquebus at you?"

Levi had been running all day after being shot at by the first firearm he had ever seen. It seemed like such a long time in the past. He shook his head to the negative. "No," he replied. The confusion was thick in his voice. "How do you know about that?" he asked tentatively.

"We saw it happen. Only we thought you were Lohman," Katrina explained.

"Yeah, they thought so too." Levi nodded his head back down the trail. Then, suddenly coming to his senses, he dropped to a knee and bowed. "Forgive me, Your Grace. I have forgotten all manners here. We must get you back to the safety of the royal guard at once."

Katrina was startled at the incongruity of the obeisance in their predicament. "I don't think you need to do that out here," she muttered awkwardly.

Levi stood, and for a moment they silently pondered the confusing situation. At length Katrina said, "There are more of those guys back there."

Levi looked up and down the trail. It was indistinct, and would disappear into shadows within minutes as the sun went down. He looked at the princess, who at that moment seemed much more like a little girl in desperate need than the second most powerful woman in the kingdom.

Katrina had a distant look in her eyes as she commented, "Marisa took my cloak, well, Lohman's cloak, and ran back to the Gypsy camp, kind of like you decoyed for Lohman. I hope she made it ... I hope ..."

"My Grace," Levi bowed again, "I know of another way out of this valley, but ..."

Reality struck suddenly, and Katrina held up her hand. "You mustn't bow or defer to me in any manner, Levi," she whispered, "If we are seen or ... caught ... they'll know I'm ... you know." Fear was attempting to take control of the girl's mind as the horrors of the potential outcomes settled in. But she was smart and forced her mind to sift through the fear.

Levi was surprised, but caught on to the implications immediately. He nodded and said, "I'll treat you as if you were my own sister."

Katrina bit her lower lip and pointed at the royal crest on the cloak. "You need to get rid of this first," she replied.

Levi shook his head. "They'll find it, and then if we get chased ..." He let his words trail off.

"You and your sister ..." Katrina almost teared up at the thought, "Actually, you should treat me like a servant."

Levi was taken aback. "But, Your Grace ..." he protested.

She put up her hand and hissed, "Katrina!"

Levi collected his wits and returned to the earlier conversation. "I can lead us out of this valley over another pass, but not in the dark. We'll have to hide off this trail for the night, in case they come looking with torches."

Katrina looked into the rapidly growing darkness and shuddered. "No fire?"

It was a rhetorical question, but it conveyed the anxiety within. Levi actually realized the girl's fears and responded, "No, but you'll be plenty warm in that wool cloak."

Katrina did not realize until the following dawn that Levi had not been nearly warm enough in the lightweight royal cloak.

Marisa

"It's Marisa! Not the princess!" The news flashed through the Gypsy camp. Within minutes, Marisa and Captain Cornelius were face to face.

"Child, where is the princess?" Cornelius snapped.

Marisa collapsed in exhaustion as many helping hands cradled her. She began to sob out her reply. "I wore her cloak so she could escape a bunch of thugs. They mistook me for her and chased me. I thought she would be here by now! She may still be hiding in the woods by the stony creek crossing. And the prince has been shot with a very large arquebus!"

Cornelius was again stunned. "Does this run in their family?" he asked no one in particular.

"Where is she?" Prince Lohman demanded as he elbowed his way through the crowd. When he reached the center, he too was stunned. "Marisa?" His eyes went to the cloak she was wearing, his cloak.

"Lohman! You've not been shot!" Marisa exclaimed.

"No, that was Levi."

"What!?"

"He wasn't hit, I think, by the speed that he escaped. How do you know about that? Why are you wearing my cloak?"

Marisa told the whole story, from wearing the brothers' clothing, slipping out of the camp for their adventure, to discovering the camp of outlaws and witnessing the shooting, to the exchange of cloaks for Katrina's safety, and the panicked retreat back to the Gypsy camp.

Oppression hung over the entire camp like a fog as Captain Cornelius paced back and forth. His quandary was obvious, as his options essentially did not exist. Finally, after about ten minutes of his muttering to himself, Cornelius stated to Samuel, "No matter what I do, keep the troops together to protect the prince, or pursue the princess, or split my force ... one or both of my charges are left at risk. A dozen of my men could attack the camp, but if the princess is captured, or there is an ambush, we would be at a severe disadvantage."

The captain paused and stared into Samuel's dark eyes. "If I take any of my men away, that leaves the prince unprotected against an all-out attack." He nodded toward the darkening woods. "You know. If they're out there waiting for an opportunity."

The captain and the woodsman stared at each other in silence for a moment, then Samuel cautiously offered, "Keep the prince in safety, and I'll go hunt for the princess."

Cornelius was frustrated. "Then when you find her, you take on fifty men?"

"I'm still working on that part, but I may find her first, and I'll take all my arrows." Samuel patted his quiver with a confidence he did not fully possess.

Cornelius knew Samuel was right, but he also knew that if something happened to either of the royal heirs, it would be his own to account for.

Grudgingly, Cornelius agreed. "You have until this time tomorrow, then I will move on another plan."

Samuel slipped into the darkening forest within a half hour.

"Peace to the king!" the rider cried out. "I have an urgent message for King Lawrence.!"

The guards already had arrows trained on the rider as the guard captain demanded, "Put your hands in view and state your name and business quickly!"

"I am Sean the Gypsy Tinker of the lineage of Gepetka. I have a message of urgent importance from Captain Cornelius for King Lawrence."

The voice from the shadows ordered, "Dismount and step away from your horse."

The Gypsy dutifully did as he was commanded, and royal guards immediately surrounded him. Sean the Gypsy was searched, and his dagger and sword were confiscated.

The guard captain stepped into the flickering torchlight and sized up the Gypsy. "A Gypsy carrying a sword seems rather peculiar. Do you know how to use this thing?"

The Gypsy's face reddened at the question. "Not really, sir, but Captain Cornelius showed me a few moves in case I needed to charge through a gang of armed thugs."

The guard captain's eyebrows arched in a slight display of disbelief. "So, how is Cornelius these days?" he asked more as a test than a query.

The Gypsy had ridden hard for over twelve hours and did not understand the captain's rhetoric. "Captain Cornelius," Sean sputtered in confusion, "is most distraught at the disappearance of the princess."

Captain Roen was taken aback. "What?" he blurted in alarm.

"I have an urgent message for the king," Sean reiterated.

Things happened quickly after that and, within a half hour, a court was assembled and lit with dozens of torches.

The king and nobles were awakened and assembled in the torchlight, and Sean the Gypsy was ushered into the king's presence.

Sean presented the written message from Captain Cornelius, and the king read it aloud.

Your Highness,

I am in a painful quandary. There was an apparent attempt to kidnap the prince yesterday morning, and by a clever maneuver, one of the Gypsies thwarted the attempt. The report from the prince as well as Samuel the Woodsman is that there are at least fifty outlaws involved in this plot.

The prince is safe in the custody of the royal guard. We have activated a defensive strategy for his protection.

I am grieved to report that the princess and a friend left the camp undetected on the same morning. Apparently the same outlaws that were intending to capture the prince pursued the princess and her friend as well. The friend returned to camp after leaving the princess hidden.

My painful dilemma is this: To split my force and search for the princess would leave the prince vulnerable in the event of an attack on the Gypsy camp. And to protect the prince as he should be, is to leave the princess.

The assembly was as quiet as a tomb for several long heartbeats. Then Queen Sarah began to sob. Lady Sylvia rushed to comfort her sister.

King Lawrence continued to stare at the parchment as if the story might change to something more palatable. Finally the king asked, "How could my daughter slip out of camp unnoticed?"

Sean waited for a moment, then realized he was the only one with the answers. "The girls put on clothes like their brothers, who were going hunting. So when they passed the guard, he mistook them for the boys."

There was a volley of questions from Lord William, the king, and the captain that Sean answered to his best knowledge.

Finally King Lawrence made his plan. "We shall send a detachment of soldiers with the women and domestic servants back to the castle at Falcon's Crest. The remainder will travel in battle trim and make all haste to convene with Cornelius."

"Agreed," William stated emphatically.

"Agreed," the captain echoed.

"Absolutely not!" Queen Sarah objected. "I'll not run away when my daughter is in need!" There was a fire of determination in her eyes.

"You are being willful, my dear wife," the king said in a polite, but terse, voice.

"And you, my love, are a stubborn man," the queen replied with more emotion and less aplomb. "And we have two stubborn, willful children who need us both at this very moment."

"My dear," King Lawrence said as he always began his final argument with his wife, "you are hardly suited to the mortal combat that will be sure to take place upon the next day or two."

Sarah looked away into the darkness without responding for several moments. She finally replied in a meek, almost melancholy, voice, "Your arm is powerful, and I know your sense of justice is already at work seeking your enemies. But my heart is dying as my imagination races through the dark forest with my daughter as she flees for her life ..." The queen let her words fall off.

The set of determination on the king's face softened at her words. He looked at the captain, who shrugged uncertainly. His eyes went to William, who was already looking to Sylvia. The king followed William's gaze to Sylvia's dampened eyes. She blinked once, then nodded ever so slightly.

King Lawrence ran his fingers nervously through his hair. "I have a sense," he spoke haltingly, "that my father would have known exactly what to do, and that Master Yomahito would have already enacted a plan, but I feel conflicted all the way to my bones."

After a brief silence, the king sent a servant to summon the priest. To himself, Lawrence muttered, "This distress is draining the marrow from my bones."

After the priest had made a prayer of intercession, the assembly was dismissed. As the council was disbanding, the Gypsy waved nervously to catch the king's attention.

"Yes, of course, what is it, Sean?" the king asked.

"Sire, there is one more thing," Sean fidgeted as he spoke. "They have an arquebus. We heard the boom."

There was again a strong silence, which the king broke. "That should give us an edge on stealth. I have a one hundred shilling reward for the man who brings me the arquebus and its deceased owner."

Two Hunters

As a generalization, the outlaws were not particularly strong on intellectual practices. In fact, a good many of them bordered on the level of fools. But they were determined to collect their prey, and they pursued relentlessly throughout that first day. None of them ever realized that the confusion in the forest was due to the fact that there were five people running away from them.

Samuel and the prince had made the best use of cover. And with their head start, they had only been spotted and chased for a brief time before they outran the thugs. They had made it back to the Gypsy camp in good time, and reported their experience to the captain of the guard.

In their respective blind rushing about, Marisa and Levi had nearly crossed paths on several occasions. That completely confused the outlaws as the sibling fugitives were wearing identical royal cloaks. Upon losing track of Levi in their initial pursuit, the outlaws had split into several groups to try to head him off, and one of those groups eventually spotted Marisa. With shouted curses, they abandoned their original path and took off after her. They were a noisy bunch, and it didn't take long for the other groups to redirect their pursuit. The outlaws never guessed that Marisa had intentionally shown herself to draw them away from the princess.

In the chaos, another group spotted Levi, quite by chance, and the whole boisterous pursuit reversed direction again. Eventually, after a series of frustrating course changes, the outlaws lost track of everyone.

When the gang wearily made their way back into their own camp that evening, they were berated violently by Jarell. After a quarter hour's worth of cursing, Jarell questioned each of the men as to what he had seen. The stories were greatly conflicted as he fruitlessly worked his way through the men. After a dozen inquiries, he had enough of it and demanded, "Did any one of you morons actually see the prince in the woods?"

There was a protracted silence before Keith volunteered, "Captain, I think he can fly. I seen him clear as day going up a south facin' hillside … thirty, maybe fifty paces away, before he disappears in the forest. Then less than a quarter hour later, Nate is screamin' at us to come help chase. He seen that prince a mile the other way."

"So you quit chasing the prince to follow Nate?" Rhenska snapped.

Jarell looked irritated that Rhenska had asked the question that was in his mind. Keith shifted uneasily on his feet before he answered. "Umm, not really. We sort of lost 'im in the forest by then."

"Lost him in the forest in a few minutes? What a bunch of incompetent jackanapes you have here!" Rhenska spat the words at Jarell.

Keith muttered, "There's a woodsman in those forests somewhere." Heads nodded assent, and several men grunted acknowledgement to the subtle statement. Rhenska met Jarell's eyes and his expression confirmed the group's sentiment.

Jarell pointed at Nate and demanded, "Did you, in fact, see the prince when you called out for the others?"

"Yes, sir. And our whole group saw 'im too." Nate had been anticipating the question.

Rhenska demanded, "Did any of *my* men see the prince when you saw him?"

There was a long pause and one of the men offered, "None of your men was with our group."

"Did any of my men see the prince during any of this day's shenanigans, or were you all napping under an apple tree?" Rhenska snapped. She knew she had lost her composure.

There was more silence as the men were afraid to speak up. Rhenska glowered expectantly. At length, one of her men said, "We, me and the boys with me, all had the same thing happen. One minute he's here, and one minute he's somewheres else a long ways off. It ain't right. I got a bad feeling about the whole thing."

"Would you like me to relieve you of your bad feeling?" Rhenska asked in a wickedly calm tone as she ominously clutched her arquebus.

Even in the inconsistent light of the fire, the sweat could be seen on the man's face as he shook his head to the negative.

"We need to plan," Jarell said as he nodded toward Rhenska. They exited the cave to speak away from the gathered men. Rhenska knew she needed to regain control of the situation. She also wanted to gain control of Jarell.

"That prince can't get back to the Gypsy camp or else we gotta overrun the guards, and they'll be prepared for us." Jarell was not telling Rhenska anything new, he just wanted to present a good front to the tired men.

Rhenska stated the obvious, "So, the boys have to go back out and find him tonight."

"Yah, I just wanted to be clear so we don't get a fight going here," Jarell grunted.

"We still have one problem that no one wants to talk about," Rhenska said.

Jarell waited a few seconds then asked, "And that is?"

"That woodsman," she replied quietly. "We've got to come up with a way to eliminate him from the mix."

Jarell's eyes involuntarily darted around attempting to peer into the shadows. "Yah. We should probably go back into the cave to work out a plan that makes sense to the guys."

Rhenska sensed his fear and realized they were both backlit by the glow coming from the cave entrance. She muttered, "Yes. Yes, and out of the night air."

The two leaders slipped back into the cave where almost all the men had returned.

Rhenska paced back and forth among the outlaws as they wolfed down their food. It had been a long day on an empty stomach for most of them. She was agitated that none the men were able to locate the prince. She was livid that their stories did not line up. But the part that was making her the most furious was that their fear of the woodsman was rubbing off on her.

That the men were paranoid about the woodsman was obvious. Every single report had included some snippet of relief that they had not encountered him. He was clearly dreaded and on their minds. How to get them to refocus on catching the prince was what Rhenska really wanted to figure out.

Jarell realized he had been following Rhenska around as she paced, so he sat down and took up sullenly staring into the fire. He had been there only a few minutes when his bowman came into the cave and sat across from him.

The bowman did not have a report since he had stayed close to the camp. Jarell had privately instructed him to keep an eye on Rhenska. Naturally his silence aroused the attention of Rhenska and she called him out.

"You, bowman. Do you have a name?" Rhenska asked as if she were calling out for a refill at an inn.

The startled man looked up at Rhenska, then back to Jarell with a quizzical expression. Jarell shrugged.

"Francis," the man replied tentatively.

"Francis, can you use that bow as well as Jarell thinks you can?" she queried as her mind raced to formulate a plan.

Again the man looked at Jarell with concern. "Yeah. I can pick a squirrel out of a treetop," Francis replied with just a hint of boasting.

"Do you fancy yourself a real hunter?" Rhenska asked a bit softer.

Francis subconsciously sat up a little straighter. "Yes. Um, yes, m-ma'am." He stumbled over the title.

Rhenska had strategically maneuvered herself to be directly behind Jarell by that time. She put her hands on Jarell's shoulders and gave the bowman an innocent pout. "Would you consider yourself better than, or at least equal to this ... woodsman?" she crooned as she gestured casually in the air with her hand.

Everyone in the cave was under her spell by that point. Francis nodded assent even as the questions welled in the back of his mind. He replied, "I've been poaching the king's deer since I could pick both ends of a bow off the ground. There ain't none better."

"Well, I've been thinking." Rhenska paused for the effect, "I'm just a girl, you know. Not a real hunter. I wish I was a real hunter so I could go track this woodsman down and take care of him myself. But you have *all* the skills necessary to do the job."

Rhenska never broke eye contact with the man. She knew she had hypnotized his ego, and she was going in for the kill. Suddenly she let her eyes get girlishly wide as she asked, "Oh! But, you're not afraid, are you?"

The man was all but slobbering at his own adulation in his newfound status. Francis came to the surface and stammered, "Oh, no. No, ma'am, not afraid."

"Oh, good. I think if you brought me that man's right arm and his bow, you could be cut in for an extra portion of the take." Rhenska patted Jarell on the shoulders excitedly, "Don't you think that's a good deal, dear?"

Jarell jumped at the shift of conversation. "Uh, yeah. Yeah, that seems fair." He spoke long before he tried to figure out where the extra share was coming from.

"Well …" Rhenska drew out the theatrical pause to appear to be contemplating. "We all know that guy is lurking out there somewhere. You should probably slip out under the cover of darkness so you can do all that mysterious woodscraft stealthiness and earn your honors." Again she paused and looked down at Jarell. "With your permission, of course? He is your man, after all. And you really should be the one making the final assessment of his capabilities."

Jarell had been so effectively mesmerized by Rhenska's tactic that he did not even realize she was manipulating the entire gang. Her brilliant play on their fear and Francis' ego had shifted the balance of power heavily into her hands.

Jarell looked around at the two gathered gangs in the cave. Their eyes were all affixed on him. Without ever having to be acknowledged, their latent fears had been summoned to the surface. In their eyes, there was either certain death or assured victory based on Jarell's decision. In a desperate attempt to save face, he tried to muster a counterproposal that sounded plausible. In the pause, Rhenska shifted ever so slightly to recapture the attention of the men.

"We do need you to approve before arrows come streaking out of the darkness." Her disingenuous smile projected her condescension. That was the instant Jarell lost control of his gang.

Jarell stammered, "Of course he's up to it. You heard the man. He's the best!"

There was a collective sigh of relief, and one man even clapped for two beats before he realized that was a concession of his own fear. Jarell looked around the cave again and, seeing the approval on the faces of the men, felt relief that he had made the right decision. He was not shrewd enough to realize that Rhenska had essentially taken over his gang. He also was not smart enough to realize that she had, with his approval, eliminated his personal bodyguard from the equation.

Rhenska pointed at Nate and ordered, "Better get a loaf of bread and some cheese wrapped up for Francis. He's got an important mission."

Nate jumped to the task, never realizing he had begun taking orders from the wrong leader. In a few minutes, Francis had been outfitted with his small bundle of food. He shrugged into his cloak and strapped on his extra quiver. Rhenska adjusted his cloak clasp and hood until everything was seated perfectly. She produced a scented hankie like a magician and tucked it into his cloak like a favor. With a coy wink, she patted his chest. "That's for luck. It's nice to have a real man around," she whispered.

With his allegiance completely transferred, and his ego at an all-time high, Francis departed the cave. His inflated confidence conveyed into his every move and, for all the gathered men, he looked like a war hero saving the day.

After an appropriate pause to allow Francis time to disappear, the gangs were sent back out into the darkness so that in the morning they could pick up their chase where they had left off.

Rhenska and Jarell were left in the camp alone. Neither actually wanted the company of the other. But great evil in the heart generates great need for company, even if it is intolerable. What Jarell did not comprehend was that their mutual need for each other was rapidly becoming unbalanced. Rhenska knew it. She had intentionally manipulated the situation for that end, and she knew it was only a matter of time before she no longer needed Jarell at all. She smiled to herself.

Escape Across the Mountain

Levi shook Katrina awake as the sky just began to lighten. "Prin ..., hey, girl," he whispered. "We've got to get going."

Princess Katrina opened her eyes, then jolted awake. "I was dreaming about a fire." She practically breathed the words.

Levi could tell by the look in her eyes that it had not been a good dream.

As they ascended the mountain through the forest, Katrina nearly forgot that her stomach was empty. She got lost in the sensations of the mountain beauty, and her mood lifted appreciably.

Birds flitted about in the dawn's first rays, filling her eyes with wonder. The aromas of damp mountain soil and budding flowers tingled her nose. And the distant tinkle of a tiny brook made every fiber of her being want to dance. She began to hum under her breath. When they emerged from the woods into an open shale slope, the panoramic scene was breathtaking.

Katrina slowed for a better look and exclaimed, "Oh, Levi, this is glorious!"

Levi paused, irritated for a moment. He looked around and acknowledged, "It is, but we should keep ..."

"That's him!" a voice shouted from down the hill.

"Go!" Levi grabbed the princess's hand, and they bolted across the remaining shale into the woods.

Violent cursing and screamed demands followed them, but the two never looked back.

When Levi finally slowed to a walk, Katrina fell to the ground, gasping. She felt like she was going to be sick, but there was nothing to throw up.

Levi urged, "We've got to keep running. I don't think those boys get out much, so they can't run far. But there seems to be a lot of them."

"Where are we?" Katrina asked.

Levi shook his head slowly. "I don't know. We've been going mostly east, maybe some north … the wrong way from the pass I wanted to cross over anyway."

"So, now what?" she asked.

"We keep going. No matter where we are, you are safer lost with me, than anywhere those villains can find you," Levi stated bluntly.

"Levi, are you lost?" Katrina asked incredulously.

Levi shrugged and sighed.

Katrina pressed the point. "If my father was here, he would identify a defensible rock formation and make a stand."

Levi's face blushed with the sting of the insult, and he retorted, "I'm neither king nor warrior. In fact, I'm not a goldsmith or tinker, either, for that matter! Sorry to inform you, but I'm just an entertainer … a jester, and there's nothing amusing going on just now."

Levi stopped abruptly and turned away. He recognized that the girl had spoken out of fear, hunger, fatigue, and frustration. "Sorry … Your Grace," he muttered.

Katrina pulled herself up and went to the Gypsy. She patted his shoulder and whispered, "I'm sorry. This is all my fault, and you're in the middle of it. And I suppose you're hungry and tired too."

Levi sighed and began to walk, "Mostly just scared. Let's go."

"You are armed with a longbow and a good quiver of arrows. Maybe we should stand and fight," Katrina encouraged.

Shaking his head, Levi retorted, "I can barely arrow game standing still. And I have no sword, and wouldn't know how to use one if I did. Our only chance is escape."

They alternately ran and walked the rest of that morning without incident. They detected no sign of pursuit as they continued down the valley. At one point, they stopped and ate some wild berries, but that only seemed to make the hunger pangs worse.

The brook at the bottom of the valley grew steadily, and they were forced ever closer by the increasingly steep valley walls. By midday they could hear a distant waterfall.

Levi stopped and pondered, while Katrina went to the small stream and washed her face and arms. When she returned, she declared, "I need a bath, but that stream is dreadfully cold. Is it possible to have a fire tonight?"

Levi's look of angst surprised the princess. He shook his head to the negative. "I think that waterfall tumbles over an old trade road by the big river. It's the only waterfall I know of in the area. If I'm correct, we're within two miles of the outlaw's camp." He let the words sink in, then continued, "I'm not sure we can even descend at the falls." Levi sighed heavily and looked back up the valley they had just traveled. "We may be trapped."

"Trapped, like there's no other path out of this valley?" Katrina asked.

He shrugged his shoulders. "I've never been in here. I've heard about it from others," he replied despondently.

She stared at the side of his face as he was struggling to decide what to do. Suddenly she felt a surge of empathy for the man. He was making life and death decisions without any training or information.

"You're a good man, Levi the Entertainer," she stated. "My father would be proud of how you are handling this situation."

Levi stared at the girl in surprise. "I'm sorry, but I think we have to go back the way we came."

Reluctantly, the princess and Levi returned up the trail they had just traveled.

*   *   *   *   *

Samuel had slowly picked his way toward the camp of the outlaws in the darkness. He had occasionally heard distant noises that were manmade, but he could not distinguish anything. He had slept for a couple of hours as the moon was setting, and continued to the outlaw's camp at dawn. He was surprised to find it abandoned.

He watched it for a short time, and was startled to see a woman emerge from the cave entrance. She grabbed an armload of wood and re-entered the cave.

Samuel was pondering the meaning of it, when a runner came crashing into the camp and excitedly delivered some news inside the cave. A man emerged with the woman and the messenger and, with some general hand motions and a few sounds, Samuel discerned that the pursuit was happening far from the Gypsy camp. He figured the man was the gang leader. He briefly considered capturing the leader, but decided that protecting the princess was the more urgent need.

With a snap decision, Samuel slipped back into the forest and, as fast as he dared travel, headed through the woods toward the east. It was not much of a plan, but it was the general direction the messenger had indicated. After he had traveled a few hours, he heard excited voices in the distance.

Samuel knew the sounds had to be coming from a valley to carry so far. He strained his hearing to get a more specific direction. There were only two likely valleys he could identify, so he took the nearest one and began picking his way up the ridge away from the trail. He saw a group of a dozen men hastily traveling down the valley. He prepared to accost them, but was startled to discover they did not have a prisoner.

Wherever is the princess if these goons don't have her? he pondered in panic.

Samuel forced his thoughts into submission and listened for more clues. To his chagrin, he realized he was in the wrong valley. In frustration, he considered arrowing the men, but he knew he could not stop all of them, and his potential for surprise would be lost. As fast as he could, he followed the group.

When the group Samuel was chasing met up with some of the others, he could hear their excited chatter. He was dismayed; they had their hostage. It was hunter's instinct, but he checked the shadows. *Just past noon,* he thought.

Samuel was not able to see their hostage, as the gang was large and rather strung out along the trail. He knew it had to be Princess Katrina, so he tried to keep pace with the outlaws as they headed back to their camp. When he was finally in a position to see the outlaw's camp, the sun was just setting behind the mountains. There was a general stir of activity, but the princess was not in sight and Samuel surmised she was being held in the cave.

Lacking a better plan, Samuel settled in to wait for darkness.

*   *   *   *   *

By the time he had been out of the cave an hour, Francis the Bowman had projected his entire life's failures on the woodsman and kindled a furious lust for vengeance. He did not understand the truth about why he hated the woodsman so intensely. Hatred is naturally the firstborn offspring of fear. But Francis had no clue how he had been manipulated by Rhenska, and he had no clue how that had set up his self-manipulation. He only knew he was determined to kill the woodsman and collect the unthinkable wealth that had been promised to him.

Blinded to anything but his own desire, Francis set out. He had originally thought to stake out the Gypsy camp, but decided the woodsman would come searching for the prince. So he had headed up into the hill country north of the cave and west of the Gypsy camp. He did not have an effective plan, but he knew he needed to do something.

Kidnapped for Ransom

Princess Katrina heard the voices first. She grabbed Levi's arm and whispered, "Did you hear that?"

Levi stopped and strained his ears. Suddenly someone yelled out, "Right there!"

Levi and Katrina turned and bolted, only to find out they had passed some of the bandits who had been hidden. Surrounded, Levi looked up the steep slope. "Let's go!"

They made no more than thirty yards when Levi was tackled. He rolled and tumbled down the hill, losing his bow and arrows in the fall. He tried to draw his dagger, but was tangled in the cloak. Within moments, he was subdued and his hands were tied behind his back.

Levi was somewhat disoriented from the tumble, so he looked around to see if Katrina had escaped. Her shriek gave him the answer.

A particularly nasty-looking man with brown teeth had Katrina by the hair and was dragging her with glee. "I got me a woman!" the vile-looking man excitedly declared as he rejoined the group.

No one saw it coming, but a brutish fellow called Lou, of Rhenska's gang, punched him so hard his feet both lifted off the ground. Lou pointed a blunt finger at the perverted man and thundered, "You listen to me, Dog, no one's got nothin' 'til Rhenska says so!"

The injured man, known as Dog, let his head settle back to the ground as he attempted to staunch the flow of blood from his nose and split lips. As he spit out a few broken teeth, he vowed under his breath that he would kill Lou at the first opportunity.

The princess was tied with her hands in front, and the two were marched back up the valley they had traveled.

Levi did his best to count, but could only guess that the dozen in front of him were matched behind. He was drastically underestimating. His mind raced for a way to free the princess, but he came up blank, so he decided to try to negotiate.

Katrina was surprised to hear Levi address Lou in an impeccable court imitation. "Good sir, you have pursued me these many miles, and now have overtaken me and my servant. To what end have you done all of this?"

Lou looked at Levi and chuckled. "I ain't the one you negotiate with, lad. Save it."

Levi persisted. "You realize that your head is at stake if so much as one hair on my servant's head is harmed. Much more so for my own person."

Lou just grunted and tugged Levi's tether.

After a time, Levi decided to try one more tack. "You know that by sunrise tomorrow, my father's army will be swarming over these hills, and no one will escape the justice of his sword."

There was some nervous throat clearing among the nearby men, and Lou stopped abruptly. Levi all but bumped into the big blunt finger that he found pointing at his face.

"Listen, boy," Lou snapped, "I do what Rhenska says. Rhenska says, 'Catch the prince,' that's what I done! If Rhenska says to cook ya' and eat ya' fer breakfast ... you'll be et fer breakfast! Now shut yer fancy talk and save it fer Rhenska."

Levi could almost feel the shudder run through Katrina. He became silent for the rest of their trek back to the outlaw camp.

*　　*　　*　　*　　*

He was only ever known as Spaniard, and he was the fastest runner in Rhenska's gang. Hours before the rest of the gang returned, Spaniard raced into the outlaw camp with the news. "We have the prince! He's trussed up and Lou's got him on a tether like a bear at a carnival!" he exclaimed excitedly.

Rhenska was delighted, as much as delight could be attributed to her. She immediately made ready to write the ransom note, but Jarell interrupted her reveling. "We haven't seen this prince yet!" he forcefully argued.

"If we don't actually have him, we can still get out of this kingdom alive. But if we send a ransom note to the king, and we don't actually have him, or he manages to escape, we're as good as dead."

She leveled a cold stare into Jarell's eyes. "If you don't want to be part of this venture, then you had best leave now. My man, Lou, has the prince, and no one messes with Lou … for long."

Jarell was annoyed at her obvious contempt for him. He turned away without any further remark.

Rhenska was decently literate, but she spoke her words as she painstakingly marked them on the parchment. "My dear King Lawrence," she began.

Jarell erupted, "You can't start a ransom note like that! It sounds like you are petitioning the Crown for a favor! It sounds like you're a …" He broke off before finishing.

"It sounds like I'm a woman?" Rhenska retorted. "I am a woman! What difference does that make?"

Jarell carefully chose his words. "It sounds entirely too polite. I don't think he will take it seriously that way."

Rhenska shook her head, "Oh, Jarell, Jarell. You pathetic, unimaginative creature, you. Trust me, he will take my note seriously." She ended with a heavy sigh.

Jarell knew Rhenska was in high spirits since she did not finish her sentence with a threat to shoot him. Rhenska continued her note,

> *Your beloved son is in my capable care. My army is ever vigilant for intruders, so do not attempt a rescue. Naturally, your son's fingers, ears, nose, and eyes all depend upon your full cooperation. I hope you understand me.*

> *He is a fine young man and will be returned to you fully intact when you deliver his weight in gold coins. Please put the gold on a horse and send it with my messenger.*

She signed the note with an "R" and waved it to dry the ink.

Jarell felt a strong sense of euphoria at the prospect of a trunk full of gold, but his skeptical nature haunted the back of his mind.

The note was neatly rolled and tied, and Spaniard was about to leave, when Jarell suddenly had a suspicion. "Hey! One of my men should go with Spaniard … to make sure he don't skip out with the gold."

"I thought we were one united group now. Like a family?" Rhenska's spoke with a low level of sarcasm. "Then again, you may be right. I may have given him instructions to hide with the gold until I arrive and split it two ways." Rhenska guessed his suspicion correctly. She patted Jarell's face. "Well, pick one of your boys that can keep up with him."

Jarell turned red, knowing none could even if they were there. He waved his hand in a cavalier gesture of dismissal, and Spaniard trotted off down the trail.

It was just about dark when the outlaw messenger arrived at the king's camp.

*   *   *   *   *

Levi immediately recognized the camp of the outlaws as they were brought in on the same trail he had been on when Rhenska shot at him. Katrina was disoriented, so she did not recognize the place. The two captives were unceremoniously deposited at the feet of a man who seemed to be in charge.

Levi had been rehearsing his ploy and spoke immediately. "Sir, your persistence is admirable. If I and my servant are released immediately, then I may have some sway with my father's wrath, and you may receive a portion of his mercy. If we are harmed in any way, you and each of your men will be hunted and slaughtered ruthlessly. No measure of torture should be off-limits to encourage any one of you to tell all your secrets."

Katrina just stared at the Gypsy as he delivered the impersonation brilliantly. The outlaws stared with mouths agape.

Jarell, the one Levi had addressed, sputtered nervously for a moment, then snapped, "Nice try, boy. But I'm here for one thing … a big trunk full of gold! And no one is stopping me from collecting it. So, if you want to keep those ears attached … you'll speak only when spoken to!"

Jarell drew his dagger as he spoke and, to the glee of his men, mimicked the act of cutting off one of Levi's ears. Levi paled slightly, and his eyes inadvertently went to Katrina.

Jarell saw the brief shift of gaze and went to the girl. With his blade, he did a slow motion mock-decapitation. "Or better yet … maybe your daddy would take this kind of gift more seriously?" Jarell's eyes never left Levi.

"No! No." The words leapt from Levi's throat. He had not anticipated that at all. "No. Please, in the holy name of heaven, please do not harm the girl." Levi was on the verge of nervous tears.

Jarell sheathed his knife and strutted very close to Levi, chuckling. "Oh, ho, ho. We are mighty concerned for a chamber girl. Now we're going to understand each other a lot better. I suspect your old man don't know about your little tryst with this … this Gypsy wench, or he'd be in fits. See, I understand the way your kind operates. So if you do just exactly as I say, she will keep her head intact, and your old man will deliver me all the gold I demand. If you try anything sneaky, well, your pretty little girlfriend will be butchered before your very eyes."

Jarell abruptly turned away for emphasis. Another idea surfaced in the greedy mind of the outlaw, and he turned back just as abruptly. "And one more thing. You are going to pay me handsomely, when you get back home, of course, to keep this little secret." Jarell pointed back and forth between the girl and Levi.

Levi stood dumbfounded for a moment, his breaths coming fast. Finally he replied weakly, "I'll pay whatever you demand." He cast his eyes down as if in shame. Then he added, "She's a resident of the king's castle, and as such, is the only person who could deliver a ransom note to my father without being immediately tortured to death."

Jarell chuckled aloud as he gleefully replied, "Your father has the ransom note by now." He looked carefully at Levi, then ordered, "Shackle the lovebirds together on the whipping beam in the cave. And bring me that lovely royal cloak."

Rhenska had remained strategically out of sight of the captives. She knew very well that plans could go astray at any moment, and her anonymity would be her best defense if everything went wrong.

Levi and Katrina were dragged into the cave. A couple of rock-rimmed fires gave poor illumination to the cavernous interior. The air was still, and the smoke rose straight up and exited through some thick foliage. The walls were covered with centuries' growth of dead vines, and the floor of the cave was carpeted with a thick bed of leaves. It was a strange cave, to be sure, and Levi took it all in as he was led to the back. A rock outcrop that looked somewhat like a carved column had an arm-sized hole drilled through it just below shoulder level. A manacle was clamped around Levi's right wrist, and the short chain was shoved through the hole. The other end of the manacle was clamped around Katrina's left wrist.

Three men had accompanied Lou to chain the captives, and one of them snatched the royal cloak off of Levi. "The Captain will be enjoying this, thank you very much," the man said cynically.

Lou looked at Levi and spied his dagger. He grabbed it quickly and nearly spat out, "Those morons of Jarell's didn't even check you for weapons! When Rhenska sees this, she'll blast someone!" And the big man laughed deeply.

Levi was alarmed. He nodded toward the cave entrance and asked, "That's not the leader?"

Lou grunted, "He's their leader. Rhenska's the real leader, the one really in charge."

The four men left the cave, and Levi felt his knees shaking. He knew nothing was certain. Katrina leaned around the whipping beam and whispered, "You were brilliant. Even if they kill us both, you couldn't have protected me any better than that."

Levi shook his head, not so much in disagreement, but in confusion. "I just can't figure out why the royal guard unit has not come looking for you. Samuel should have been able to lead them directly here." His perplexity was evident in his voice. Then he added with chagrin, "He doesn't get lost."

Katrina was at a loss. Her imagination generated a hundred horrible happenings to her brother that would have the guard unable to leave the camp. She could not conclude anything cohesively, and let her mind rest on the subject. "They will come when my father arrives," she stated, knowing fully that it was at least two days before the king was expected at the Gypsy Jamboree.

Levi kept silent a long time before he said, "Sooner or later, my ruse will be uncovered, and then I'll be put to death. I fear dreadfully for your welfare." He took a deep breath, then, with a painful quaver in his voice, added, "This is probably a good time for us to make our final peace with the Almighty."

They both fell silent with their own thoughts as they watched the foliage at the top of the cave slowly fade to darkness.

Before the light was completely gone, the two gangs gathered into the cave to escape the evening dew. Levi was able to do an accurate head count after that. He came up with forty-seven. He knew there would be a few guards posted. *Fifty!* he thought. *Fifty men are going to be impossible to defeat. Maybe I can confuse them.*

The outlaws built up the fires to ward off the damp cold of the mountain night air, and the improved light helped Levi assess the place.

Spaniard

King Lawrence had pressed his caravan as fast and far as the animals could travel in the rugged hill country. Their projected travel allotment was ten miles per day with the entire accoutrement and entourage. That day they had traveled eighteen. Everyone who was not mounted on a battle horse was tired. The cooks were particularly worn out, as they had rushed about frantically trying to quiet the incessant rattling of cookware in their wagons. It had not been a pretty day of travel.

They made camp just a few miles shy of the ferry crossing, at a place where, under normal circumstances, Sylvia would have experienced a sort of thrill of anticipation. On that occasion, she felt an intense sense of cold dread.

The camp was erected a bit more spartan than normal, but by no means in battle trim. All the main comforts for sleeping had been set up, but the dining tent, chairs, and table were foregone. The cooks hastily made a fire and cooked a much simpler fare than would normally accompany a royal outing, but the king had insisted on simplicity.

Shortly after the meal was served, there was a disturbance at the far guard post. A man could be seen speaking to the guard, then their voices were raised, and the guard took the man to the ground forcefully. The guards erupted into action, and all hands were mustered for defense. Numerous other guards ran to the assistance of the far guard and, within a few minutes, the visitor was surrounded by soldiers and being questioned by the captain.

All of the events took place out of sight of the royal diners as they sat amid the sleeping tents. They had heard some distant commotion, but no alarm signal had been raised, so they were unconcerned.

There was a good deal of surprise among the king's party when the captain approached the gathering. He was recognized and nervously asked for a private audience with the king. King Lawrence looked around those gathered and asked the captain the nature of the business. He shuffled a bit and explained, "We have a ransom note for you from a man who claims to represent a vicious gang of thugs. They claim to have the prince in their custody."

The king leapt to his feet, as did all the others. "All non-council members leave us now," Lawrence ordered. There was a general scurry as people hurried away from the king's gathering. The king looked at his wife and knew before he said anything that she would not leave. He glanced at Sylvia and saw the same defiant fire in her eyes, and abandoned the argument before it was begun.

"Show me the note," Lawrence ordered, and the captain handed it over. He read it silently and, with a slight hint of dismay, handed it to William.

William read it and looked up swiftly at the king. "They think they have the prince? How well did Katrina disguise herself?"

The note was read aloud to the others, and they all pondered the conflicted information in silence. At length William mused, "We need to question the messenger."

"Yes. Yes, that is the only key we have," the king responded. "Bring the messenger."

In minutes, Spaniard stood insolently before the king. The guards forced him to the ground, and the guard sergeant demanded, "You will bow before His Majesty or I'll break your legs!"

When the man was raised to be questioned by the council, he sneered, "Your boy will be getting equal treatment by ..."

No one saw the king move, but his boot planted squarely in the man's face. Spaniard was thrust so violently to the ground that both guards lost their grip on his arms. The guards swiftly regained the man's arms, but he was as limp as a rag. There was a general scurry, and the king, red-faced, turned away and confessed as if to himself, "Forgive me, dear Lord above, for that is the first time in my life I have delivered vengeance in anger."

Sarah rushed to his side and, through tears, consoled, "I think we all felt the urge to do the same thing."

William, his blood pumping vigorously with the sudden rush of anger, blurted in awe, "Whoa! That was amazing. Master Yomahito would have been proud."

Sylvia shook her head slowly. "I want to drive a dagger into his chest for the horrors that are happening to my niece, but we do kind of need this man alive to tell us where she is."

The king, regaining his composure, turned back and asked the guard captain, "Is he dead?"

The captain looked the king in the eye and, with newfound reverence, stated, "By some miracle, he is alive. But not very. His teeth are all gone, and his nose and skull are crushed, and … I'm not sure about his neck …"

The king held up his hand and the captain stopped his pre-death autopsy of the man. "Get this man some wine, now," he ordered. "We need answers, and he should be delivered to the gallows intact."

A servant rushed up with a chalice of wine and, with the help of a guard, they managed to get a little to trickle into Spaniard's mouth. There was a weak sputter and the man's eyes opened about halfway. William got close to the man and asked, "Where is the prince?" He paused to let the man realize the gravity of his situation before he continued, "You can die easy or you can die very, very hard. Where is the prince?"

The man rolled his eyes and whispered through his mangled face, "We got him and his girlfriend in a secret cave."

"Girlfriend?" William asked rhetorically, then demanded, "Where is the cave?"

"You can kill me, but the king knows. He knows his brat has taken up with some cheap Gypsy wench. He can't ever unknow that now." The man began to cough after his exertion.

William was irritated by the man's rambling. He demanded again, "Where's the cave?"

Spaniard attempted to speak, but faded into a stupor. William glanced up at King Lawrence, who looked as forlorn as a whipped dog. Everyone was holding their breath, waiting. William realized they were all expecting him to make a profound statement. He averted his eyes for a moment, then decided to give the king the only thing he had. "He will never give us true information about the location. We can hang him now or try again when he comes back around. If he comes back around."

The king was stunned. "I fear I have killed him," he all but stammered.

"No. I suspect it's better if he dies before he has a chance to play with your mind and Sarah's heart. It could be like a cat plays with a mouse," William tactlessly stated.

Sylvia cleared her throat and gave William the stare that reminded him there were others present. William looked around and corrected, "Queen Sarah, I meant to say."

King Lawrence asked the question on everyone's mind. "So what does it mean?"

William had instantly put all the clues together and realized the dreadful truth. In an attempt to formulate a good way to spin the news, he replied, "It means they have Levi and think he's the prince. And they have Katrina and think she's his Gypsy girlfriend. They are playing their roles well, I am sure. Katrina, because she is filled with imagination. And Levi, because, well, because that's what he does. I can't think of a better person to pull that off."

Sylvia quietly scolded, "William, there are many servants and soldiers hearing you refer to the queen and princess by common names."

The king looked around at the surrounding staff and stated, "Gentlemen, for the duration of this crisis, please excuse my brother-in-law and sister-in-law for using the names we speak to one another in private. I'm sure you all understand, and can keep a confidence."

There were some awkward, "Yes, Sire," statements, and everyone returned to their business.

"How long do you suppose they can keep up their ruse?" Sarah asked weakly.

Shaking his head, William mused, "I expect they could keep it up indefinitely. As long as no one identified either of them."

Stir Crazy

The time one spends in waiting is multiplied exponentially in the mind when a great distress is afoot. On the first day after the messenger was sent to the king, Captain Cornelius had militarized the Gypsy camp.

The carts were arranged as a sort of barrier around the vulnerable side of the camp. Gypsy boys and girls were conscripted as lookouts on rotating watches. And anyone with a weapon was given instruction on its use. They were not much of an army, but it was the resource Cornelius had at his disposal, and he utilized it to the best advantage.

The prince had been appointed as the sword and staff instructor, and for the majority of the day, he had been surrounded by students. It was a bit surprising to Prince Lohman that some of the men were readily handy with a sword, even if they were not proficient.

Having ordered the area for defense and arranged his network of civilian guards, Cornelius temporarily promoted each of his soldiers to command a small detachment of Gypsies. By nightfall, he felt the infrastructure was as orderly as he could obtain in the circumstances. And at that point, he nearly lost his sanity.

Preparing for anything, even inescapable calamity, is by far easier on the mind than awaiting it. And Captain Cornelius wanted, with every fiber of his being, to take the battle to the enemy. Only he did not actually know who, or even where, the enemy was. Consequently, he was forced to wait.

All day, the captain had anticipated Samuel's triumphant return. But in his trained mind, he knew better than to hope for anything easy. When the darkness had fully settled in the mountains, Captain Cornelius allowed himself a rest. He had not been asleep for long, or particularly well, when the alarm was raised. A rider was spotted passing by the outpost fire.

It turned out to be Sean with a return message from King Lawrence.

The weary rider had put on many miles in the saddle that day, and could hardly stand up when he finally arrived at the Gypsy camp. Several guards assisted him, and a Gypsy took his horse to rub down and turn into the pasture.

Captain Cornelius ran in a most undignified manner to the guard post to question Sean. He found the Gypsy sitting on a stump eagerly slurping down a bowl of hot soup. The Gypsy made to stand when the captain approached, but Cornelius motioned him to remain seated as he blurted, "What does the king desire for us to do?"

The Gypsy messenger handed a note to the captain as he replied, "The queen refused to turn back, so the whole company is coming this way as fast as they can travel."

Cornelius processed the information as he broke the king's seal and unrolled the note. He leaned close to the fire and read it aloud as several of his soldiers gathered around.

Captain Cornelius,

The present situation is uncertain as there is no evidence to suggest that Katrina is at immediate risk. I and my company are making haste to come to you. We should be there by nightfall one day early. Trust Samuel to do his craft. Make any arrangements with the Gypsies to keep Lohman safe. I will arrange payment for all they do.

Your diligence in service is testimony to to your faithful character.

Respond in code if any further developments arise.

The king's signet ended the transcript.

After staring at the note for a few extra minutes, Cornelius muttered, "I will surely lose my sanity while waiting."

He had no sooner made his statement when one of the guards hesitantly called out, "Captain?"

Cornelius turned to respond but was taken aback. The man, who was staring off to the southeast, was clearly unnerved. There was a low-level pattern glowing like embers in the sky. It was too symmetrical to be natural, but had an ominous look as if there were illuminated eyes in the sky.

Betrayed

The two guards had become paranoid by the prisoners' whispering. The larger guard seemed to take it personally. By his clothing and long matted beard, the man had not bathed in a very long time. Theo, the larger guard, whispered, "The prince don't worry me none. It's the way that Gypsy wench tries to look you in the eye that makes my skin crawl."

"She's a kid, she can't hurt you, ya lug!" Nate spat with derision.

"She can put a curse on you in a minute if she catches your eye! Turn you into a frog or some other insect, she can!" Theo defended.

"Frogs ain't insects, you fool!" Nate refuted.

"They are!" Theo insisted.

"You can look it up in a book! Frogs ain't insects! Ask the prince, them folks got books that tell everything!" Nate challenged.

"Ain't nuthin' in books but spells. I seen one, an' it didn't say nuthin' to me. Just had wizard marks in it!" Theo replied.

"Frogs ain't insects."

"My ma, rest in peace, cooked up the best frog soup ever I ate. An' she said a frog was an insect! It's an insect!" Theo was getting irritated.

The two guards sat sullenly after their collective intellects were exhausted. They occasionally glanced at the captives with a mixture of fear and suspicion.

*   *   *   *   *

The cave was only dimly lit when Harold, the spy, arrived. He took in the scene quickly, and sat as far away from the prisoners as was possible. He carefully positioned himself so his back would be toward the prince. He knew if the prince saw his face, he would be identified as one of the king's hostlers, and his life would be worthless if he was found out.

By chance, he had met Jarell in a tavern one evening when Harold was well under the influence of a large quantity of ale. The notorious outlaw had seduced the king's hostler with the promise of easy riches and complete anonymity. Harold had fallen for the rash promises, and his intention had been to get a share of the ransom and slip back into his regular life without ever being implicated. As he looked furtively around the cave, the brutal reality began to set in on the young hostler that nothing is ever that simple.

There was a general din of conversations as the men huddled around the two fires in the cave. They were eating whatever rations anyone had thought to bring, and the general demeanor was subdued. The earlier euphoria that had swept through the camp when the ransom note had been sent had all but worn off as they nervously waited for the king to send the trunk full of gold coins. Each man also knew, in the back of his mind, that there was an equal chance that the king's guard could sweep in at any moment as well. The waiting was insufferable.

The conversation by the guard fire had been bordering on idiocy, but no one intervened, even when heated voices were raised. However, when Harold heard the prince call out to one of the guards, his heart momentarily stopped. Something in his mind raced through all the possibilities, but nothing made sense. It was the wrong voice.

Discreetly, Harold turned to get a glimpse of the prince. His size was right, but his posture was wrong. Harold slowly stood and casually circled around the outer edge of the cave. He tried to stay out of the light until he was close enough to see clearly. He stood, mouth agape, for a moment, before he whispered, "That's not the prince."

Katrina noticed Harold at his soft gasp. "Harold? Have you come to rescue us?" she whispered.

They made eye contact for an instant before he averted his eyes from hers. In near panic, he rushed to

Jarell and hissed. "Captain Jarell, I need to have a word with you, sir!"

"Speak on, man. You look like you've seen a ghost," Jarell coaxed.

"Not here. Alone." Harold nodded toward the darkened gateway. "It's really urgent!" The man was quivering.

Outside the cave, Jarell snapped, "This had better be important!"

"Yes, it had better be," crooned Rhenska, who had silently followed them.

"Without her." Harold nodded toward Rhenska as he spoke.

"That's a strong demand for a mute," she sneered as her accusing eyes never wavered from Jarell's.

Jarell shrugged off the insinuation.

Rhenska calmly patted Harold's arm, "Not without her. We don't keep secrets here, darling."

"Just what the devil is it?" Jarell spat out impatiently.

Harold's voice almost broke into a whimper. "That's not the prince."

Jarell grabbed Harold's tunic as his hand closed around his sword. "What do you mean? If this is some kind of trick, I'll gut you alive!"

Harold was visibly shaking. "No trick. I swear it on my mother's grave! This is really bad. He's not the prince."

Rhenska motioned with a nod of her head toward the cave and demanded, "Then who is he?"

"I don't know. Some random Gypsy, I suppose," Harold managed through chattering teeth.

Jarell and Rhenska stared toward the lighted entrance, processing the ramifications of the news.

"It's worse," Harold sniffed. "The girl ..."

"What about the girl?" Rhenska snapped.

"She's the princess! We're all going to be quartered!" Harold choked out.

Rhenska perked up. "Well, that's some good news. The princess should be worth a trunk full of gold too."

"You don't know this king. He'll hunt us relentlessly 'til we're all dead," Harold whispered.

Rhenska turned to Jarell and calmly ordered, "Kill the Gypsy and this coward immediately. I'll handle the negotiations with the king."

A bright flash and muffled boom startled them. They whirled toward the cave entrance in time to see a panicked exodus of men lunging through the doorway. Fire was glowing eerily through each of the overhead vents creating ghostlike lights in the low clouds. Several of the men were smoldering, and Theo was engulfed in flames. There was complete chaos with everyone yelling in panic as they futilely attempted to put out the fire on the filthy man.

Within minutes, everything inside the old citadel that was flammable was burning. Jarell frantically screamed orders to get the hostages out, but no one could enter against the flames.

One man kept running to the doorway and calling for Roland, but there was no answer, as his friend had not gotten to the entrance in time. He ran about in shock repeating, "How can a stone cave be on fire? How can a stone cave be on fire? It's witchcraft! It's witchcraft!" until someone clubbed him and knocked him out.

Harold bolted into the dark forest, hoping he would not be missed in the maelstrom.

It had taken only a few seconds for Katrina to realize that the hostler was a conspirator with the criminals. She leaned around the pillar and, in a frantic whisper, hissed, "Levi! They are going to kill you. We have to do something, now!"

For some reason, Levi was surprised by the passion in Katrina's voice. "What? Why?" he replied in confusion.

"That man is one of the hostlers at the castle stables. He knows me and Lohman. He knows who we are, and he's talking to the leader right now." The princess nearly lost her composure as she spoke.

Levi looked at the ground and muttered, "I just wish I had my own cloak."

Realization struck them simultaneously. "Is my trick bag in the hidden pocket on the left side?"

Katrina's left hand was the one shackled, so she groped awkwardly around in the cloak. "You carry a lot of stuff in your cloak," she muttered absently as she pulled out items from several pockets.

"Well, Marisa should have known enough to empty all that before you went out," Levi retorted. "I just need the linen bag and the small dagger."

"We have a weapon?" Katrina gasped.

"No, it's barely longer than my hand, but it is wickedly sharp," Levi replied as if he was deeply distracted.

Katrina handed him the knife, and he discreetly maneuvered it to his shackled right hand. The hole through the pillar where they were secured served as a handy place to conceal the small blade.

As she slipped the bag into his hand, Katrina whispered, "The guards are staring hard at us."

"I need you to trust me." Levi spoke in a tone that Katrina had never heard from him. "Do you feel the breeze coming from behind?"

Tentatively she answered, "Yes." She had not noticed it before.

"We're in the old citadel. That leads to the river. Can you smell the water?" His intensity began to frighten the princess.

"You mean this cave is the ..." Katrina's words were sharply interrupted by Levi.

"Listen!" he whispered urgently. "This contains a dozen of my flash powder juggling balls. When I toss this bag into the guard's fire, I need you to push your arm as far through the hole as you can reach. We will have about a one minute diversion to make our escape. When the fire erupts, you race down the cave. Just keep going face into the wind. You'll get out."

"Levi! That knife will never sever this chain!" Katrina's voice had gone too loud.

The shorter guard looked over and demanded, "Hey, what's that about a knife?"

Levi held out the bag and said, "No knife here, just a cloth cursed with the black death." He tossed the bag deftly into the fire and the guards recoiled away from its path.

The pause lasted about two heartbeats, then the short guard stood and made a step toward the prisoners. Levi tugged the chain and hissed, "Now!"

Katrina's slender arm obediently came through the hole in the pillar. Her creamy soft skin all but glowed in the firelight. Levi bared the razor sharp blade of the knife and called out, "Forgive me, princess!"

The blade flashed swiftly and blood showered them both. Katrina screamed in shock and, an instant later, Levi's bag of flash powder exploded, launching burning embers throughout the cave. In seconds, fire was everywhere.

Shock

Nate, the guard, was burned badly, but he had gotten out of the cave alive. Jarell, who was never known for his compassion, grabbed the traumatized man by the shirt and shook the hapless man as he hurled questions.

"What do you mean he cut the Gypsy girl's arm off? You idiot! How'd he get a weapon?" Jarell glanced aside in disbelief at the burning cave. "She wasn't even a Gypsy, you fool! She was the princess! You let that sneaky Gypsy kill our hostage?" The circular questions and accusations were clear indicators that Jarell was in shock.

"I think he was a wizard, Captain Jarell," Nate whimpered. "He made witchcraft happen with his words. Maybe he planned it all along."

Jarell unceremoniously dropped Nate to the ground and whirled on Rhenska. His sword came to hand as he shouted. "You plotted all this with that Gypsy, you witch!"

Rhenska lowered her arquebus at Jarell, but the wick was not burning. His lip curved into a sneer at her, and in that instant, she realized he knew the limitations of the firearm. The gathering outlaws all drew their weapons and rapidly rallied beside their respective leaders. Some of Jarell's gang seemed to be confused about whom they should align with. The air was thick with mistrust and angst.

"Where is he taking her? This is some of your conjuring, and don't try to deny it!" Jarell was yelling even though they were mere feet apart.

As the two confused gangs faced down in the flickering shadows, there was a protracted silence between the leaders. Finally Rhenska spoke. "Jarell, I hate you to the end of time. But I have no earthly idea what just happened in there."

Jarell was as startled as the rest of the men, for it was undoubtedly the first true statement Rhenska had uttered in years.

Rhenska asked, "How much do you trust your spy? Maybe that really is the prince?"

Jarell hesitated only a second, then called out, "Harold!"

There was no reply.

A quick survey of the assembled men proved Harold was not present. Jarell looked at Rhenska quizzically. They were both at a loss, but neither wanted to admit confusion in front of their gangs. Rhenska hedged, "We either need to get our hostages back, or we need to clear out of this kingdom tonight. The instant either of those two get to the king's men, we are all marked for death."

There was a general stir amongst the thugs, and fear became palpable in the questions and whispered conversations. Jarell snapped, "I came for a pile of gold!" He thrust his sword back into its sheath with a snap. "Those two are huddled in that cave waiting for the fire to die down. They can't escape if we guard the door."

"What if they're dead?" someone asked.

Again there was an uncertain pause. Finally Rhenska answered, "We'll know in an hour or two. The fire is already burning out."

The fire was indeed burning out. In the remnants of long dead vines and leaves, the fire had spread swiftly. And, like kindling, it was dying down swiftly as well.

Jarell had regained his composure and ordered no one in particular, "We need them both alive until we know if we have the prince or the princess!" Everyone nodded assent as the situation became more clear to the men.

The balance of power that had shifted heavily to Rhenska was again destabilized. Jarell's ferocity had restored some degree of his men's respect. Rhenska was perhaps the only one who was aware of it, and she had no intention of letting Jarell reclaim any authority. She announced, "Whoever kills that traitor spy, Harold, if that's his real name, gets his portion of gold. He must not get back to the king's men either."

"First light, I want ten men on his trail!" Jarell snapped. His deep paranoia overwhelmed his abhorrence of Rhenska at that moment. It did not occur to him until much later, that he had endorsed her hit on one of his men.

Wake Up Call

The muffled voices of the guards carried concern as well as confusion. Lawrence barely distinguished the words, "Should we wake him?" and he knew something was afoot.

"He's awake. What is it?" King Lawrence called out softly through the tent wall. He had been unable to sleep more than a few minutes at a time since the news came that his daughter had been kidnapped. His mind generated nightmares that he could not sleep through.

"What is it?" Sarah sat up quickly. She had been trying to remain still so Lawrence could sleep.

The tent guard replied, "Sire, there is a fire in the hill country nearby. It appeared suddenly and is casting unnatural lights into the clouds." He paused for a long moment, then added, "We don't all agree on what it is or what it means."

By that point the king and queen had exited their tent to see what was the cause of such speculation. King Lawrence voiced the obvious. "The fire is not visible, but the light seems to be emanating from many sources."

They observed in silence for a moment before the camp barrier guard asked, "Is that the camp of the outlaws or is that the Gypsy camp?"

Sylvia and William had slipped up silently behind the preoccupied group. Sleep had been elusive for them as well. Sylvia startled everyone when she answered, "That is … in the hills near the Old Miller's Ford. The Gypsy camp would be further west, to the left, a few miles."

Sarah had always found comfort in her sister's presence. She looked at Sylvia and asked, "What does it mean?"

A strange look of comprehension slowly showed on Sylvia's face. "It means, the citadel that was lost for two centuries is now found."

"What?" the king snapped. "Is this some riddle?"

Shaking her head slowly, Sylvia replied, "I think the kidnappers have camped in the old citadel, and somehow have set it on fire. See the symmetry in the reflected lights? Those must be from the hidden windows. Air vents, really."

"Does that mean Katrina is in a fire?" Sarah blurted without thinking.

Everyone was silent for a long time. They watched with their fears unvoiced as the reflecting fire slowly dimmed and eventually disappeared altogether. The camp guard advised, "Majesty, you and the others should get some sleep. Tomorrow will have its share of troubles."

As Sylvia turned back toward their tent, she found that she was standing alone. "William?" she called out instinctively.

King Lawrence stopped mid-stride, holding the door flap to his tent open. He looked back at Sylvia's silhouette. "Is he there?" Lawrence asked, knowing the answer as the words passed his lips.

Archer on the Hunt

The reflected fire in the low clouds gave William a perfect reckoning. He knew there would be a limited time, so he rushed the first few miles, which were on the old trade road. As he neared the area of the fire, the road had degenerated from years of disuse. He knew there would be a hidden trail, but finding it in the dark would be impossible. The woodsman took the best fix he could get on the dying reflection, then slipped into the forest and found a place to rest until daylight.

While he had been trotting up the road, William pondered with slight remorse about leaving the king's camp without permission. He did not think the king would have any objection, but he knew Sylvia would. It had been easy enough to slip into the shadows and sneak past the guards. William hoped the guards would not be disciplined for not seeing his exit. He could sneak by most guards without being detected. The truth was, he had done so frequently, and returned with game in the same manner. This time, of course, it was different.

William slept better that night than he had since the first news had come to the king about the missing princess. Perhaps it was the workout of running, or possibly the act of engaging rather than awaiting the unknown. As the sky began to glow with the mountain sunrise, William woke up. His mind was well-rested, and his senses all came alive as the information of the prior day was reviewed. He listened for a long time before stirring.

When he finally began to move, William's mind was engaged as the hunter. Had the kidnappers known what was in the woods that morning, any of them with sense would have fled immediately. For the most deadly predator in the region was on the hunt, and they were the prey.

It was midday when William found the trail. It had been camouflaged well with cut branches where it intersected the road, but the leaves on the branches were hanging at an odd angle. It was an effective way of cloaking a path, but once a man sees it, he cannot unsee it.

William was careful to leave no trace of his passing. He did not expect the outlaws to be searching for him, but he wanted to be completely invisible until necessary. Traveling near, but off, the trail was slow. It did eventually lead William to the camp. He had heard distant shouts and calls throughout the day, but had not actually seen the outlaws. When he could finally see the camp, it was abandoned.

Observing the scene of the camp from a hidden vantage, William began to reconstruct the events that had transpired in that place. The opening to the cave was visible, with soot-blackened stones serving as a great beacon. The ground was trampled into patterns where men had been gathered. The remains of a couple of men had been hastily covered with dirt at the edge of the forest. One had been fairly tall. Even from that distance, William could tell the men had died in the fire.

Something had gone terribly wrong in that camp. What had caused the disturbance was not apparent, so William pondered his options. As he sat contemplating, two distinct motions came into his senses.

The first, on the opposite hillside, turned out to be a man sneaking through the underbrush. His complete lack of stealthiness indicated he was inept in woodscraft. His furtive scanning indicated he was hiding from someone. *Thrashing buffoon*, he mentally labeled the man.

The second was more subtle. It took a while before William realized there was another human in the area. He could not detect the motion, but eventually he recognized a false pattern of sounds. He realized someone was simulating the sound of small woods creatures to disguise his own movements. *The silent stalker is good*, William determined, *very good*.

He was not sure if the silent stalker was hunting the thrashing buffoon, but William decided that unless any of their drama revealed the location of the princess, he would not intervene. He did, however, string his bow and pulled an arrow from his quiver.

The day was waning when the silent stalker finally came into view. The noisy buffoon had moved on, and it was apparent the stalker was not interested in that man. At first there had been the slightest motion through the underbrush. William readied his bow just in time to get an actual glimpse of a cloak. When the silhouette of the man could be distinguished, William noted that he carried two quivers of arrows. The stalker paused and examined the scene of the camp. *This man has been well-trained,* William pondered with some concern.

When the stalker turned to look around, William drew his arrow, then nearly gasped aloud.

Trial by Fire

When Levi came to, his head felt like it was on fire. He wondered briefly why he was even alive. The pain from his right hand was excruciating. He wanted to look at it, but could not muster the will. It took a few seconds for him to realize the citadel was on fire, and he was somehow propped against a stone deeper in the cave. His mind raced through the memories.

He remembered cutting off his thumb and being surprised to see the shackle slip over his maimed hand exactly as intended. He remembered the screams of panic as the room had erupted into flame. He remembered the mortified look on Katrina's face as she realized what he was about to do. He remembered feeling dizzy and falling. Suddenly he panicked. "Princess?" he cried out. Then he recalled he had instructed her to run to save herself.

"I'm right here," Katrina called out from around a corner. There was urgency in her voice.

Levi was momentarily confused. Katrina was not fleeing, but was closer to the flaming room than he was. His confusion compounded when she sprinted around the corner with the dagger glowing red, held with a thick wrap of her cloak.

"I'm so sorry, Levi," Katrina sobbed as she grabbed his arm, and in one deft motion cauterized his hand which had been bleeding excessively. Levi blacked out again.

*　　*　　*　　*　　*

When Levi came to the second time, Katrina was half-supporting, half-dragging him deeper into the cave. The wind was strong in their faces, as the fire was rapidly consuming a lot of fuel. His hand had been bound, and the pain was beyond description.

Katrina was urging him along, and Levi realized she had been doing so just to get him moving. He staggered on obediently, but was pathetically slow. They traveled a short distance in near total darkness, and Katrina decided to stop. She again propped Levi into a corner and, as he faded off to sleep, she sat trying to listen against the low moan of the wind blowing up the cave. Eventually the wind died down and Katrina fell asleep.

Superstitions

"It's still choking hot in there," Nate insisted. "No one could have survived in that fire."

Rhenska demanded, "Go in and find the prisoners! It is not that hot!"

"What if the Gypsy girl can cast a spell? What if she has magic? She may have survived the fire by magic! It ain't safe to go in there!" Nate urged. His superstitions fed his imagination.

Jarell pointed into the entrance and snapped, "You survived that fire! Go find them!"

Nate looked hesitantly from one leader to the other. He seemed about to bolt for the woods.

Rhenska wanted to slap the man and inform him that his imagined magic was mythical, but part of her control strategy was to maintain a persona as a sorceress. She whispered in a friendly way, "That's a good point, but witches are executed in fire, because it is the only spirit they cannot survive." She patted his face gently and, with an endearing wink, added, "You have demonstrated such powerful resistance to fire, I shouldn't be surprised if you had a gift of your own."

The man was dumb, there was no question about that. Though his fears ran deep, Rhenska's manipulation worked, and slowly he edged into the burned-out doorway. When he got near the back of the chamber, he found the badly burned body of a man. He took it to be the prince. He was shaken by the stench. At the pillar where the hostages had been chained, there was nothing. He realized the fire had not burned the back of the chamber, and that pushed him over the edge.

Rushing out through the doorway Nate all but shrieked, "She's done it! She set the place afire with her spell and burned up the prince in it! Then she just disappeared! That place is haunted! Haunted!"

Jarell snatched the torch from the man and shoved him aside. His initial fear was that there would be some kind of trap awaiting the first person into the cave. He was confident Rhenska suspected the same thing. Not wanting to wait for her lead, he ducked into the chamber and began his own search. Rhenska followed immediately. It only took a minute to locate the dead man. He was clearly armed with a leather fighting vest, a sword, and an old battle helmet.

Jarell tried to remember the man's name. He had been one of Rhenska's gang. The name escaped him. Rhenska stated dispassionately, "Roland." They moved to the back of the chamber where the pillar stood. It was of stone with a hole carved through it from some ancient past. It was also intact with no sign of the prisoners.

In the eerily flickering torchlight, the two outlaws stood dumbfounded. A number of the braver men had gathered around them, and it became evident something extraordinary had transpired. Finally, Jarell muttered, "Maybe it is haunted."

As a unit, the men all turned and made their way to the door. Rhenska pointed at their deceased companion, and a couple of men dragged him out of the cave. While everyone else rushed to get out of the cave, Rhenska made a protracted inspection of the place. Jarell stood in the entrance trying to hurry the woman out, but she was not going to let the moment pass.

When she finally emerged, Jarell knew his manhood had been publicly humiliated by her prolonged visit inside where the men had feared. The look of awe the men had for Rhenska was universal and undeniable. Jarell wanted to do or say something, but he was at a total loss. He dropped to sit on a stump of wood and muttered, "We got to catch them two."

Rhenska patted his shoulder reassuringly and replied, "Sleep well, boys. I've got a plan. Tomorrow will be a busy day. But we will be rich beyond measure."

She did not have a plan except to gain control, but it worked and, from that moment, everyone, including Jarell, deferred to Rhenska. The gangs slept fitfully outside the cave that night.

Samuel

The smoke from the cookfires stung Samuel's eyes as he peered into the cave. He had waited until well after dark to sneak up to the stone vents for a look inside. He was not expecting so many outlaws inside, but he was rewarded by spotting the princess and Levi together. He could make out that they were shackled to some kind of post in the shadowy back corner of the cave. But he could not see much more. He tried to hear any conversation that would give him a clue, but could discern nothing of value from that sense either.

Assessing the situation, he knew it would be folly to attempt a straight out rescue. There were simply too many enemies and one tiny cave entrance. He briefly considered hiding and picking them off one at a time, but he was afraid that Levi or Katrina would bear the brunt of revenge for that type of assault. He examined the structure of the stone vents. They seemed like naturally occurring openings in the cave chamber roof. Sometime long in the past, small boulders had been strategically placed to block the view in or the light escaping. It was a perfect fortress. He concluded it had to be the old citadel, even though it was full of long dead leaves and vines.

Samuel pondered the old legend. Some great ancestor of his had been in the citadel when it fell to invaders. He remembered she had escaped out a secret passage that led to the river. Two hundred years is plenty of time for a cave to collapse, he knew, but Samuel decided the best chance was to find the cave at the river and sneak in for a rescue. He had no better plan and could not imagine leaving Katrina and Levi alone. He slipped off into the forest for the night.

Getting to the river in the dark turned out to be easier than he had anticipated. The old road, though it was hardly used for two centuries, was more obvious by night than it was during the day. The opening between

the mature trees marked itself nicely even in the cloud-
diffused moonlight.

For Samuel, it had been a long, stress-filled day
pursuing the ever-changing sounds of the chase. He was
dog-weary, and wished he had thought to grab some
extra bread and dried meat. Hungry and sore, the bed of
moss he found captured him for a much needed sleep.

*   *   *   *   *

Somewhere in his dreams, Samuel heard an unearthly
moaning. It grew in intensity and made the hair on his
neck stand up. Ever so slowly, he arose and strung his
bow. He could not reason why he did so, for he felt
certain the sound was emanating from the netherworld.
Slowly he stalked the nearly sub-audible moaning. There
was a slight motion in some shrubbery, and Samuel
demanded, "Show yourself! In the name of the king!" He
drew his arrow to his cheek in one fluid motion and,
failing his command, Samuel shot into the center of the
moving bush.

Nothing happened but the sound of the arrow
ricocheting and echoing. *Echoing?* Samuel's stunned
mind took a moment to grasp the significance. *The cave!
Of course, the cookfires would be used as warming fires
in the night. They would draw lots of air.* Samuel
carefully entered the cave and began to creep up into it,
but it was simply too dark to travel, especially with a
bow and full quiver.

He rested the remainder of that night hidden just
inside the entrance to the cave.

91

Plan Change

Rhenska had originally intended to murder Jarell during that night. But the turn of events changed her mind. She knew they needed every person to hunt down the prince or princess. At first light, Rhenska ordered the men into search parties of five each and sent them out. The charge was to recapture their missing hostages alive, but the hostler, Harold, was to be killed.

There was urgency in their mission, and it showed on the faces of the two gang leaders. Jarell had let Rhenska make the plans and orders, in part because he did not know what to do. He detested her even more than before when she seemed to effortlessly lay out the new strategy.

Jarell had made one major contribution. He had chosen their alternate gathering place. It was the unidentifiable ruins of what had likely been a wood chopper's home in times long past. The place was up the mountain toward the north and was not far from the old road. It was not as defensible as the cave, but they had all become uneasy about the cave.

After the men were dispersed onto their quest, Jarell led Rhenska to the new gathering place. It was not much of a victory, but it made Jarell feel better to have some perception of control.

When they arrived, Jarell made a fire inside the walls of the dilapidated structure. They began to pace impatiently as they awaited any news. They did not have to wait for long.

Four men came racing into the newly occupied camp. One of the men breathlessly reported, "We were ambushed!"

"By who? Where? How many were there? Where's Frank? Were they mounted? Did you morons actually lead them here?" Rhenska's questions erupted in a staccato fashion.

"Frank went into the bushes to … to take care of business, and he sudden like fell back with an arrow in his head!" The spokesman paused to formulate the ending. "Then we just barely got away before they broke out of the forest after us."

Rhenska exploded with rage. "You ran from one arrow!" She berated them vehemently, questioning their gender, their mothers' integrities, and their very humanity. The men stood and took the abuse without blinking.

When Rhenska paused, Jarell interjected, "Was the archer with the prince or princess?"

There was a momentary hesitation before one of the men muttered, "We never saw them. They just seemed to be in the forest."

Rhenska turned red and was about to go off again, but Jarell grabbed the opportunity to try to take control. "They're hiding something in that place! Find another group and get back there fast. Sneak up on it from two sides. Don't let the princess get away!"

"Where was this?" Rhenska snapped.

"On the road near the river. There was a little trickle of a creek that we walked across," the group leader replied nervously.

Everyone paused momentarily. Rhenska ordered, "If there were many of them, they would have run you down. Francis is out there hunting that woodsman, so you'll be safe. Go quickly!"

*　　*　　*　　*　　*

Samuel had awakened late. His natural sense of time had been distorted by the complete darkness of the cave and his own fatigue. When he tried to sort out the direction he should travel, he felt a bit claustrophobic. So, intending to get some fresh air and sort through his thoughts, he had crept toward the faint glow of light that reflected poorly into the cave. When he got to the mouth of the cave, he was surprised to hear men trampling on the road discussing the debate about the prince and princess. He stepped back into the shadow of the cave and slowly drew an arrow.

He listened to the men discuss the circumstances of their search. When he heard the words, "They've escaped clean," Samuel was ecstatic. His mind raced through the implications. He knew they could not have gotten too far in the night. He could not imagine how they had managed to get out of the cave. He also presumed they were not safe if the gang was still searching for them.

His one-man council was unceremoniously interrupted when he heard a man say he was headed into the underbrush to relieve himself. Samuel drew his arrow just as the man broke through. Wide-eyed with discovery of the cave, the man opened his mouth to call out to the others. He never saw Samuel. He never knew what hit him. The force of the arrow thrust him back through the shrub thicket and the rest of the gang fled in panic.

Samuel was about to pursue them, but realized they represented only a small group of many who were searching for the princess. He did not comprehend why they were confused about her identity, but he knew he had to find her first. He retrieved his arrow from the dead man and decided to search in the opposite direction the men went. He presumed they were retreating to where they had come from. He also presumed that was where the princess was not. It was not a great strategy, but it was the only information he had to go on.

*   *   *   *   *

Horrifying nightmares plagued Katrina's sleep. Somewhere in her subconscious, she forced herself to wake up to end the dream. When she awoke, the stench of burned flesh was the first thing that greeted her senses. She gasped at the realization that nightmare and reality were intertwined.

She remembered Levi and reached for him. In the darkness, her hand found his hand, and he shrieked in pain. "Oh, no! Levi!" was all the traumatized girl could choke out. Shakily, she helped him to his feet. He was gasping in pain and she was shaking with shock when they heard voices echo in the cave.

She pulled Levi close until her lips almost touched his ear. She breathed the words, "We must flee silently. Hold my arm."

Obediently, Levi followed step-by-step as Katrina painstakingly picked their way deeper into the cave. The light breeze in their faces gave her direction, but did not help with where they stepped. They took a few tumbles, and each time Levi insisted she go on without him. Her heart ached for him as Levi shuddered with pain. She could hear his teeth clenched against the urge to groan. Each time she would coax him up with the insistence that she would not leave him.

After what seemed an eternity, Katrina thought she saw a glow ahead. At first it was elusive, like a mirage, but eventually became more evident. Her spirit lifted considerably when the cave was actually discernible to her eyes. As they drew closer to the light, Katrina stumbled on a stick in the cave. Something about it was out of place, so she picked it up and discovered, to her surprise, that it was an arrow.

She carried the arrow, taking comfort that they possessed a weapon, although she had no inkling of how she could use it. As they came to the mouth of the cave, Katrina gasped.

Levi, though semi-delirious, asked, "What is it?"

"Samuel's arrow!" she whispered excitedly. "Samuel is nearby!"

"We're rescued?" Levi murmured.

Katrina looked at her cousin in the light. There was so much more blood on him than she had realized, that she suddenly despaired. For the first time, she realized that Levi might not survive their ordeal. "Almost, Levi. Almost," was all she whispered before turning her face so he could not see the tears welling in her eyes. It was a harsh way for a young girl to be forced to grow up.

Katrina weighed the next decision without discussing it with Levi. She discarded the idea of making a straight-out run for the Gypsy camp. She was too uncertain of which way to travel. She could hear the sound of the river, and debated making a run for her father's camp. She knew the royal party would be heading up the road to the Gypsy Jamboree. The part she did not know was how far away he was. She knew they would be the most vulnerable on the road. At length, she opted to travel in the cover of the forest, as slow as Levi needed, to get back to the Gypsy camp.

Katrina had no sooner come to that conclusion, when a group of about ten men went tramping past. Each man jumped over the muddy trickle and never looked aside. They were only briefly visible through the brush, but she could tell they were part of the gang.

With a shudder, she led Levi away from the cave entrance into the underbrush that stood between the hillside and the road. They had gone scant yards when the men came rushing back to the little creek.

"This was the spot!" one of them declared excitedly.

"Can't be! Where's Frank?" another voice challenged.

"Maybe they're carnivals?" a droll voice offered.

There was the sound of someone getting hit as another voice derided, "Idiot! Cannibals, not carnivals!"

"This is it, all right. They got rid of the body. Let's spread out and rush through the thicket all at the same time," someone ordered. There was a general preparation before the rush.

Katrina's knuckles were white as she gripped the arrow in anticipation. They had slowly ducked down and were huddled together, uncertain of even what to expect. Ever so slowly, she wrapped her arm around Levi's neck with her hand near his mouth. She hoped against all odds that he would not gasp when there was sudden motion.

The rush came with a shout, and the gang hurtled through the underbrush with a terrific racket. The nearest one nearly stepped on Levi's foot, but he was so intent on breaking through the foliage he did not see the hiding fugitives.

Levi had understood Katrina's gesture and had braced
himself against reacting. It had worked, and the two
remained motionless except for the incessant shaking of
Levi. It was evident that he was suffering badly from his
injury.

The gang all convened at the cave entrance, and a
great discussion ensued. They entered the cave only far
enough to be considered inside. Their words carried
clearly to Katrina. In the end, they decided to leave four
guards at the cave and report back to Jarell and
Rhenska. By the time the thugs emerged from the cave,
Katrina had led Levi far enough away that they could
sneak through the underbrush.

Once clear of the immediate threat, they rushed
through the forest in a generally northern direction.
After they had traveled a mile, Levi collapsed at the
base of a tree and gasped, "I cannot go any further.
Leave me. I am holding up your progress."

Katrina knelt beside him and felt his forehead. He was
beginning to fever and she knew he would get worse.
She looked around and contemplated their plight. "I
can't leave you behind as long as there is some hope.
You must come with me. Besides," Katrina paused for a
long moment before confessing pragmatically, "I'm lost."

Levi slowly sat up and, with sticks and blades of grass,
began to construct a crude map of the area. "I am not
the best guide in these parts," he muttered, "But this
will get you a general lay of the land and roads."

Breakfast with the King

"Is everyone else going to starve?" the king asked
rhetorically. He had always been annoyed when his
guests were late to the table. In the camp there was no
table, but the royal party was gathered in a circle, and a
cook's helper was serving them their food.

Sylvia was embarrassed that it was her family that
was absent. It was out of character for them to miss
meals. She looked at her two youngest children. They
were alert and ready to eat. "Where is Elise?" she
whispered to the children a bit too tersely. Her stress
was evident.

Everyone knew that William had left the camp in the
night, although no one had seen him go. That fact both
annoyed and comforted Lawrence. He wished his guards
were capable of catching Lord William, but he was
pleased that the most stealthy man alive was in the
woods, searching for his daughter.

Sylvia had not actually expected an answer, but Gavin,
the eight-year-old, looked at the ground, pouting.
"Gavin?" Sylvia asked.

"She wouldn't let me go with," Gavin muttered. "She
said I was too little."

"You didn't try to stop her?" The absurdity of the
question struck her as the words left her mouth.

Sarah exclaimed, "Elise followed William into the
night? Sylvia, what is she, seventeen years of age? This
is no time for a child to be gallivanting into trouble!"

The two sisters were nearly worked into tears when
Lawrence intervened. "I recall you two were pretty
young when ..." His words trailed off with the unfinished
story. "I have no doubts that she can take care of
herself."

King Lawrence paused, then called his guards to
attention. "Did any of you see, hear, or even suspect that
someone was leaving the camp last night?"

There was no answer. The men all stood expecting a
berating. The lieutenant in charge offered, "Sire,

Captain Cornelius has said on many occasions that Lord Archer moves like a ghost. Sire, I'm bold for speaking up, but the captain never misses anything."

To the astonishment of all present, King Lawrence nodded assent and replied, "We are a fortunate people to have Lord William as our friend. You are dismissed."

"Elise!" William gasped in a low whisper. The girl drew an arrow as she spun. She stopped mid-draw when she realized it was her father. "Whatever are you doing here?" he blurted.

"I came to find my cousin," Elise replied determinedly. Her intense emotion was evident even in her hushed tone.

"How did you get out of the camp?" William asked incredulously.

"Same way you did." She shrugged.

"But I watched for a quarter hour to make sure I was not followed," William insisted.

The intensity of her expression softened for the first time as Elise smiled. "Father, you trained me. I knew you would do that, so I waited a half hour."

William was stupefied momentarily. Finally he muttered, "You're just like your mother."

"Hmm, she says I'm just like you," Elise retorted with a smug grin.

William looked at his daughter. He was emotionally conflicted between pride at her accomplishment and concern for her safety. "This could get very dangerous. I need you to stay out of trouble."

"I'm coming with you. My cousin is out there, somewhere, and she needs us," Elise insisted.

"This is my duty as a sworn guardian of the kingdom. You're not in the sworn service of the king!" William argued.

"Da, you're the one who always says ability is tantamount to responsibility." She paused and stared deeply into his eyes. "You would be here, sworn duty or not. Wouldn't you?"

William knew he could not answer her question without giving in.

"I'm coming with or going alone, but I'm not going back," she stated.

"Elise, putting yourself in jeopardy does not help the situation," William reasoned.

"I've got two quivers full. I'll be fine," she replied.

William's mouth opened to protest, but he found no words. He had spoken those exact words to Sylvia many times. They had always been intended to give Sylvia the ultimate degree of comfort. But he realized, in that instant, that this declaration did not convey the reassurance he had always assumed it should.

"There doesn't seem to be any activity in the cave, but I feel like I should check it out, just to be sure," William stated to bring them back to the intended mission.

"I'll go in with you," Elise replied.

"No, you stay here until I get back," William insisted, knowing as he said the words she would not stay behind. Before she could reply, he held up his hand. There was a sound in the distance that had caught his attention.

Elise's eyes widened. "That is some kind of horn or whistle," she whispered.

They strained their ears and heard it again. Elise hissed, "That's not anything in the king's service."

"They've spotted Katrina! North and a little east in the hills. Past the cave and maybe as far as the river," William deduced the direction. "Let's go!"

William and his daughter paused just long enough to look inside the burned cave and see there was no one inside. In a glance, they were both convinced it was indeed the old citadel. Elise put it into words. "For what it's worth, I think this really is the citadel from the ancient legend." Then they bolted off in the general direction of the whistle.

Friend and Foe

The good news about a signal is it summons your allies. The bad news is, it summons your enemies as well.

Samuel heard the whistle, and knew instantly it had to be the signal of choice for the outlaws. A whistle takes only breath to blow a note, while a horn requires some skill. He was close to the source, but could not see anyone.

Frustration had been boiling over in his mind for some time. Samuel had been berating himself for not being able to locate Katrina and Levi when the signal was sounded. Sprinting in the general direction of the sound, the woodsman shed all caution. He was ready to do whatever amount of battle necessary to recover the princess. In moments, he came up short on the precipice of a cliff.

He heard the whistle again, and his eyes found several of the outlaws struggling up the opposite hill. He followed their projected travel and spotted Levi lagging as Katrina pulled him along. Samuel looked for a clear target, but the distance was way too far. He drew on the leader of the chase and, in that instant, his mind heard William's first exhortation, "Focus on the spot you want the arrow to strike."

Samuel did not remember releasing the arrow in the longest shot of his life. He did not see the arrow streak away. He did not consciously compensate for the cross breeze or the two hundred paces' distance. He simply concentrated on the stain that marked the tunic of the leader. For an indeterminate number of heartbeats, everything moved slowly in Samuel's eyes. Then the arrow stuck into the man, and he was thrust face-first into the hill he was climbing.

The arrow pinioned the stain, and the man shrieked in pain. His writhing caused him to tumble backward down the hill, disrupting the others. In seconds, the whole group had slid and tumbled back down to the trail. They were mulling about in confusion when Samuel's second arrow whistled in. It was still a long shot and very much down hill. That arrow tore through one man's ear and lodged in the thigh of the man who had been originally shot.

The outlaws bolted, leaving their dying companion behind.

As Samuel cast about for a good way down the hill, he heard more whistles. His first thought was that Katrina and Levi had been spotted by another group. But he realized the sounds were coming from the wrong direction. *Reinforcements*, he thought. *I've got to get to them before the outlaws do!*

Before Samuel got to the bottom of the hill, he saw two more groups of outlaws hurry past. They were in groups of five, and both groups stopped to confer with the wounded man. The man was beyond help, but no one even offered to pull the arrows. To Samuel's dismay, the man's gesturing sent the rest of the outlaws up the hill to continue the chase. He regretted not putting a final arrow into the man. Wryly he thought, *Lord William would have put one in his eye.*

Before Samuel made his next move, a distant motion caught his eye. He could not locate the movement by looking in the exact direction, but when he turned his head, he detected it again. *What or who is up there?* he wondered. It was in the underbrush on the same side of the hill that he was on, but still at a considerable distance. His musing was disrupted by an arrow swishing by his shoulder.

Samuel dropped to the ground and slipped into the underbrush. *Who is hunting me?* he wondered in alarm. He debated momentarily whether he should go after his attacker, or continue on the trail of the princess. A whistle blow made the decision for him. He rushed down the hill through the cover of the forest. His mind tried to analyze the shot that had been taken at him. *It had to be the outlaws. They somehow know I am a threat. But how did the man see me? And it had been a long shot. The bowman is good.*

A whistle was sounded not too far away, and Samuel stopped long enough to locate the source. There were several men milling about as if they were trying to decide which direction to go. Samuel made the snap decision to give them a new kind of surprise. *Random arrows!* he thought. *No two from the same place.* And with that, he shot an arrow into the man in the group that held the whistle. Then he ran again.

*   *   *   *   *

Rhenska was livid with anger. "Your men seem to make a habit of fleeing from one arrow!" she chided Jarell. "Maybe they should learn to flee from one blast from my staff!"

"Two arrows!" the man with the shredded ear insisted. "And they came from nowhere!" He was holding a handful of blood-soaked dirt to the wounded ear.

"Shut up!" Jarell snapped at the man. Through clenched teeth he commanded, "Do. Not. Speak. Again!" Jarell was violently angry. He was embarrassed that his men had fled. He also knew Rhenska suspected foul play, since her man was the one that was arrowed and left for dead.

The three others stood nervously. They knew they were in trouble for retreating, but they were clueless about what to do. In the distance, there was another whistle. Rhenska looked in the direction of the sound. "That's not too far away," she mused aloud.

One of Rhenska's runners came into the camp at that moment. He ignored Jarell and reported directly to Rhenska. "We heard 'im! We heard the prince, only he's not the prince. He called the girl 'Princess.' And she called him Levi. We're chasin' the princess. Is that okay?"

Jarell interrupted, "You heard them talking, but didn't capture them?!"

The man glanced dismissively at Jarell, but replied to Rhenska, "They gave us the slip. I think there's some

104

devilry afoot with that Gypsy." His eyes shifted nervously. "Devilry."

"Tell Blake to put an arrow into that Gypsy and get me the princess! I expect delivery by noon!" Rhenska ordered.

The man never looked up from his agitated fixation with the ground. "He tried. That girl snatched that arrow right out from the air. We all seen it. It would have stuck the Gypsy in the chest too."

Jarell smirked, "Francis wouldn't have missed."

The man looked up at his leader as if searching for some brilliant explanation. He added, "'Twas a perfect shot and only about thirty paces."

Rhenska was speechless.

Without hesitation, Jarell snapped at his men, "Kill the Gypsy, bring me that princess, and don't come back empty-handed like these losers, or I'll kill you all!"

The wounded man whined, "What about my ear? Do I have to go?"

Jarell's ire was instantly rekindled and he half drew his sword as he snapped, "How about I take your whole head off, you idiot!"

The men raced off, leaving Jarell and Rhenska to glower at each other. Rhenska picked up her arquebus and lit the wick. She gestured in the direction of the retreating men.

Jarell's eyes narrowed suspiciously. "What?" he asked.

"No one else seems to be capable of thinking about where those two are going. When they get to that river, they will have to turn upstream or down. So you're going to pick one direction, and I'll go the other." Rhenska seemed to have thought the entire scenario through quickly.

Jarell listened for a clue. He had the sudden avaricious notion that he could get the ransom for himself and ditch everyone else. He tried to conceal his thoughts, because he still harbored the fear that Rhenska could read his mind. "I'll go downstream," he replied cautiously.

"Fine. I'll head upstream. That gold is nearly ours," Rhenska gloated a little too gleefully.

William and Elise had altered their direction as the sounds of the chase dictated. They were at an impasse at a fork in the trail when they heard the boom of the arquebus. They listened for further clues, but none came. Elise looked at William for enlightenment, but his perplexed expression told her he had no ideas.

"Do we go that way?" Elise asked uncomfortably.

"I ... I'm not sure," William replied.

A whistle was heard. William snapped his head to the direction it came from. "They're still chasing that way! If they continue, they will be cornered in the narrow valley by the waterfall. We need to cut them off." He paused, mentally calculating the travel times. "Why are they headed toward Falls Valley?" he muttered. Then, answering his own question, he replied, "Because they're lost."

Elise was surprised at the speed her father could run. Breathlessly she asked, "Why are we going this way?"

"There's a ruined farm up here that gets us to a good path into Falls Valley," he panted. "We've got to make time."

"So we are headed toward the boom?" she asked.

"Just by luck," was all he replied.

They pushed hard for a half hour before they came to the edge of the farm ruins. The field was trampled down more than William had expected. Carefully they examined the wooded border around the overgrown farmyard before entering the open space.

Elise drew an arrow and nocked it to the string. William's eyes asked the question. "Something is evil about this place," she whispered.

William knew enough to take a cue from his daughter's instinct. He nocked an arrow, and they cautiously proceeded. They had taken no more than a dozen steps when they saw the shape of a man on the ground. With a quick survey around, they hurried to the scene.

The man was quite dead, with a gaping wound in his back. The dead man's tunic had been cut open and a large letter 'R' had been carved into the flesh. William draped the loose tatters of the man's clothes over the macabre wounds. He nodded grimly, confirming what Elise presumed, that it was from the arquebus shot they had heard. The signature 'R,' he assumed, was associated with whomever had signed the ransom note that had been delivered to the king. William did not mention that.

"They're killing each other?" Elise asked.

William drew up the sleeve on the man's right arm, revealing a series of skin markings. "This was their leader … Jarell the Butcher. He was known and wanted in several kingdoms."

Elise looked around nervously. "What does this mean?"

"They have another leader. And he is either smarter or meaner than Jarell was. Maybe both. And he has an arquebus," William paused before he finished his thought. "And we are very close on his heels."

They slipped into the cover of the forest before William explained, "An arquebus is not accurate over a great distance. And it is laborious to reload. When we encounter the man with that weapon, I'll try to draw his fire at a distance. Then we'll pin arrows in any part of him that is not armored. I'm sorry to put this burden on you at this age."

"Da, I'll be fine," was all she replied.

The Great Escape Plan

Levi had made a pretty good map of the region. He had made a few guesses, including the location of the old citadel. It was mostly accurate, but there were some obstacles on the way that he knew nothing about. He was almost relieved to be giving Katrina a plan. It was certainly not his forte, but he felt as if she had a running chance while he distracted their pursuers.

"Head up in the direction north, like you are going to the waterfall," Levi instructed.

"Where we got caught?" Katrina asked with concern.

"Kind of, but more west. You don't want to get that far down that valley before you cross over the ridge. Otherwise you will get stuck in there like we did," Levi replied.

"Okay," she muttered hesitantly with some concern.

He looked up at her and coaxed, "You can do this. When you get in the valley, on the other side, there is a stream. It's a hard climb down, but you can make it. When you get to the stream, follow upstream. It will lead you back to the Gypsy camp. There are some marshy spots along the way, but you can get around those by climbing the bank a little."

After Katrina nodded her acquiescence, Levi continued, "The only place you have to be really careful is crossing the trail. I never realized before, but it must be the old road that went to the citadel. Anyway, look carefully before you cross it so those guys don't see you."

He leaned back against the tree and looked up at her. "Go! It's just a few hours. You can get there way before dark."

Katrina knelt beside him again and whispered sternly, "Levi, you are not staying behind. I will not leave without you." She stood up and pulled on his good arm until he got shakily to his feet. "We have an escape plan, let's make it happen."

*　　*　　*　　*　　*

They made it less than a half hour before being spotted crossing the trail. The five men that had left the cave to report back to Jarell had, by chance, come around a turn and saw the pair looking for a place to climb up the hill on the north side of the trail. They had blown the signal whistle and rushed the two fugitives.

Levi and Katrina had been nearly a mile away from the outlaws when they began to run up the trail. It became obvious very quickly that the gang was going to overtake the pair, so they clamored recklessly up the hill. They were struggling toward the top when a great ruckus erupted behind them. Katrina glanced back in time to see their pursuers tumbling down the hill. "Run!" she urged, and continued to drag Levi through the forest as fast as they could go.

They heard several whistle replies, and tried to veer away from the direction of the sounds. It did not take long for them to get lost. When they found themselves at the edge of a steep bank, Levi collapsed on the ground. "Go, Princess! You have to go!"

"Levi!" Katrina's voice was forceful. "I will not leave you! I command you to continue!" She made a little stamp of her foot out of frustration. But she knew he would die with one more night of exposure.

Levi dragged himself to his feet again, and a noise caught their attention. Looking back, they were surprised to see five startled gang members looking at them. One of the men was a bowman, and he quickly drew an arrow and shot at Levi.

Katrina instinctively snatched the arrow from the air and broke it across her knee in one fluid motion. The shocked gang members gawked for a moment too long. And in a move born of quick wit and desperation, Katrina grabbed Levi and pulled him over the cliff. They tumbled through the brush for a few yards and dropped to a ledge overlooking the valley.

They were out of sight completely by the time the gang members got to the edge. Levi and Katrina held

109

still as the men excitedly argued about what to do next. Katrina felt as if her heart was going to beat itself out of her chest. When the men left, Levi finally whispered. "I hear the waterfall. We've gone way too far east again."

"Now what?" Katrina asked in near panic.

Levi pondered a moment. His head was pounding from shock and exertion. Finally he answered, "I think we need to go down to the bluff along the stream. We will be really close to the falls. I've never been on this side before, but I think we can follow the bluff back upstream until we can get across at the ford. Then we can head to the Gypsy camp."

"If we go down, will we be able to get back up? Katrina asked.

Levi looked up and mused, "I don't think we have a choice."

The princess looked up and down the valley. There was actually no trail on the side they were stranded on. "Levi, I think we should go downstream."

"Toward the waterfall?" he asked, confused.

"Yes. If no one goes there, it may be our best chance of hiding until my father arrives."

Levi processed all their options. In his wounded condition, he missed the simple failure in her logic that they had been seen going down into a valley that had only one exit. It would be only a matter of time before they were found and cornered. Deliriously he replied, "Okay."

*   *   *   *   *

The king's camp was nearly packed and ready to move out. It was to be the final day of travel, and the Gypsy camp would be their stop for the night. It was a beautiful morning with crisp air and clear skies. If it had not been for the crisis they were under, it would have been the most pleasant of days.

There was a pall of expectation over the group. No one could put their feeling into words, but they all felt it.

Captain Roen came to the king with the news. "Sire. The prisoner has come to. Would you want to question him further?"

Everyone stopped their chores and all eyes turned to the king. He slowly looked up from his preparations. His mind raced with a thousand questions and emotions colliding. "Yes," was all he could say.

When the prisoner was brought before the king, the Spaniard had a whole different persona. His one eye that was not swollen closed had a vacant stare. He clearly did not have long to live.

The king immediately demanded, "Tell me where you are holding the prince. And what is the name of your leader?"

The stupefied look in the man's face indicated he was not following the swift demands. King Lawrence was infuriated, but the captain intervened. "Sire, I think he is beyond that kind of interrogation. May I take over the inquiry?"

The king irritably agreed, and Captain Roen dismissed everyone from the immediate area. He then took one of the queen's maids and gave her a chalice of wine with the instructions to ask how to get him back to his friends.

Around the corner, Lawrence, Sarah, and Sylvia listened to the whole thing. They exchanged questioning glances that expressed their doubts at the captain's plan.

The maid nervously sat beside the man and gingerly helped him sip some of the wine. She used a warm damp cloth to wipe away the blood from around his mouth. As she did so, she whispered, "What is the best way to get you back to your friends?"

He was delirious from the head trauma, and his garbled reply was mostly indiscernible. The three words that could be interpreted with some confidence were "river," "cave," and "Rhenska," although no one understood that Rhenska was a name.

When the king and his captain conferred afterwards, they both agreed that they should not move from the existing site. They were camped near the crossroads of the trade route and the old river road that had essentially been abandoned for centuries. It paralleled the river, and they had agreed that there was no better vantage than at the crossroads.

The captain had ordered the guard to be on battle stand-by, and the men had each set their armor and weapons at the ready. The horses were saddled and prepared for prompt response to the anticipated command. Captain Roen sent two riders to the Gypsy camp to apprise Captain Cornelius, and they settled in for the insufferable wait.

The king inspected the camp and realized it was a pathetic example of a battle camp. There were far too many cooks and servants milling about with their daily chores, making life comfortable for the royal party. The presence of the queen with her maids and Lady Sylvia with her two younger children made the king nervous. After pacing about for a while, he directed the captain to arm the ladies and the servants down to age twelve.

Gavin was sullen that he had not been given a sword. He donned his quiver and kept his bow strung all day.

*   *   *   *   *

Rhenska had felt a high degree of certainty that she no longer needed Jarell to contain his men. It had been fairly easy to take charge of them in his presence. In his absence, she assumed it would be a simple matter. When she murdered him, she had every expectation that most of the plan was back in place. Her conscience had long since been seared, and she knew killing another one or two of his men could be all it would take to get the rest to comply with her will.

Her primary confidence was in Lou, her number one man. He was big, strong, brutal, and would do her every command. He was also relentless when set on a task.

112

The Vulnerable Prince

Peter had followed Jarell around for two months, since the day the famous outlaw had conscripted him. They had met on a country road where Peter was pushing a wheelbarrow load of vegetables and cheese to the village market. After several thankless years of hard work on his uncle's farm, the outlaw's romanticized view of easy riches seemed like a prime opportunity. The youth had given the food to Jarell as his payment for the "buy in" and had not looked back.

Peter was not a particularly bright fellow, and had not realized he had been played as a fool until that moment of truth when he stood over the lifeless body of Jarell. The huge hole in the back of the late outlaw was unnerving. The lad had seen Rhenska do that before. But the "R" carved into his flesh as a signature was mortifying. The lad's stomach turned and, at that instant, he decided to flee.

It had been obvious early on that Rhenska was taking over the control of the whole operation. Her men began to run roughshod over Jarell's gang. Most of the men fell in line and took their orders from Rhenska and, vicariously, from her men. However, some of Jarell's men resented it strongly. Jarell had become a mentor to Peter, and the youth had naturally gravitated to Matson and Joel because of their loyalty to the leader. It was their report to Jarell that the youth was carrying when he discovered the murder. He made the snap decision to warn them.

Peter rushed to deliver the news of Jarell's death to his comrades, but when he arrived, there were two of Rhenska's men in the group. The tension was obvious, and Peter blurted out, "Rhenska's murdered Captain Jarell, and she means to kill us all and keep all the gold for herself!"

One of the men from Rhenska's gang reached for his sword, and Matson kicked him hard in the groin. The other man grabbed his whistle, but Peter tackled that man. Joel jumped on the man Peter had on the ground and gave him a double-fisted punch to the face. Then the three comrades fled blindly into the forest.

When they had run for ten minutes or so, they had to stop for a breather. Peter excitedly described the horrible scene of Jarell's murder, and they all swore to get revenge. They had no food or money, but Peter suggested they could get back to his uncle's farm, which was in the northern portion of the kingdom.

They had a brief consultation on the subject, but none of them wanted to actually work for a living. The youth suggested they could get fed and maybe even get their clothes mended. Then they could steal his aunt's milk cow to sell for money. The plan sounded as hopeful as any other they could field, so it was agreed upon.

Just before they began to move again, Peter asked, "Are we still part of Jarell's gang, or do we need a new name?"

Each of them immediately suggested their own name as the new gang moniker, and they very nearly came to blows arguing about it. Then Joel, who was the most articulate of the bunch, suggested, "We should call us, 'Jarell's Revenge.'"

They all instantly liked the name and swore allegiance on the spot.

Joel, taking control of his tenuous lead, pointed and said, "That way's north. Let's get going."

None of them were particularly good as navigators, but they managed to generally travel north. They encountered what looked like a road, and followed it until they heard a noise as if from a large gathering of people. As it turned out, they had approached the Gypsy camp.

The men were famished, and the smell of the seasoned Gypsy food was too great a temptation to resist. The outlaw trio gathered as close as they could to the barricaded wagons, and hatched a plot to steal some of the food and then escape into the woods. As they were working up the nerve for their brazen daylight raid, one of the Gypsy guards spotted them.

With a call for help, the guard launched over the barricade and confronted the men with a pike. The outlaws had been so absorbed with their plans to fill their stomachs that they were taken completely by surprise. One of the outlaws, Matson, reached for his sword, and the pike was thrust, rather unprofessionally, into the man's forearm. He let out a shriek as several of the royal guard entered the scene. In minutes, the men were bound and dragged before Captain Cornelius.

The captain was elated to have some action to direct his men to. But when he interrogated the men, both Matson and Peter looked to Joel. It was immediately obvious to Cornelius who the spokesman was. He turned his attention to Joel and demanded, "In the name of the king, I demand you give an account of your doings and goings."

"Sir," Joel begged, "we are travelers from a distant land, and we have been robbed of our animals and all our possessions. We have no intentions of harm to this ... group of people. We have traveled a good many miles with no food to sustain us, and now we find ourselves trussed up like bandits in a strange place. Please allow us the mercy to beg food from your company here. Then we will be on our way back to our homeland."

Cornelius was very stressed and, finding no proof to link the men with the outlaw gangs, he ordered them to be unbound and fed. The Gypsies seemed to mostly ignore the men as they wolfed down the hot soup. But for some reason, the prince wanted to see the travelers for himself. They had not been particularly convincing, and he just wanted a closer look.

The instant the outlaws saw the prince, their deeply held avarice took hold of them. They exchanged shifty glances, and without so much as a second thought about how they would escape, lunged at the prince.

The hapless brigands may have had a chance if the prince and royal guard had not been on edge for over a day. Peter was the youngest and fastest. He was farmboy strong, and grabbed the prince by his left arm. The prince responded immediately with a right fist into the temple. That punch happened to be on the good side of Peter's face, and he went straight to the ground.

As the burly youth hit the dirt, Joel tackled the prince, and Matson, even though he was wounded, would have grappled his arms, but the royal guard swarmed them. In moments, the three outlaws were unceremoniously trussed again and interrogated harshly.

The outlaws would not confess to any connection with the gangs. When questioned about the princess, they would not even make eye contact. Their silence enraged Lohman, because he was sure they could shed some light as to the whereabouts of his sister. When the frustration became unbearable, the captain and the prince stepped aside to consult about legal practices.

They both agreed that the men should be hanged. Prince Lohman was convinced if they hanged the first one who attacked him, the others would give up information more freely. The problem was, they knew the prince did not have capital authority outside a direct edict from his father. And the captain was not entirely sure what authority he had to pass judgments, since they were not under an officially declared war. They mused about the rule of law, and were certain that if Lord William was present, he could pass judgment. In the end, they were stumped.

In the meantime, the Gypsy Queen and several of the elders had listened silently as the captain and prince discussed their dilemma. When at length they were finished, she spoke up. "I believe I can be of assistance to you if you would like."

The captain looked at the frail old woman and almost dismissed her, but reconsidered, and asked, "It seems unlikely, but how do you suppose you can get them to talk?"

"If you give me five minutes to prepare, then do exactly as I say, I believe two of those men will tell you everything they know. I'll do them no great harm, then you can hang them properly when the king arrives," the old woman replied.

Captain Cornelius wondered if he was losing his grip on sanity for even considering the old Gypsy's offer. He looked at the prince. The prince was looking back with the same degree of uncertainty.

"How long 'til they talk?" Cornelius asked briskly.

"Oh, just a few minutes, I suppose," was all the woman replied as she walked away.

"Okay. I guess. Yes, okay." The captain was clearly out of sorts.

As promised, the Gypsy Queen returned in five minutes. She carried an ancient brass censer with smoke billowing out of it. Captain Cornelius wondered if it had been stolen from a church, but thought better of asking. She neither looked left or right, but went straight to the men, who were tied to separate trees. The old Gypsy slowly walked around each man while swinging the censer and wafting smoke into their faces. She chanted something that was indiscernible, but sounded like an incantation.

A crowd of Gypsies gathered to see the spectacle, and the guard became visibly ill at ease. The captain was about to ask what she was doing, when she abruptly stopped in front of the one man in the gang who was not injured. "What is your name, child?" she asked eerily.

His face paled as the black eyes of the Gypsy Queen seemed to penetrate into his soul. "Joel," he managed to croak out.

She nodded and all but whispered, "Bring this one. I will divide his spirit in two."

The captain nodded to a couple of his men, and Joel was taken from the tree and led by a tether. He squeaked in a rather unmanly way, "What is this? What is happening?" And thus the guards dragged him slowly away as they followed the Gypsy Queen through the camp.

The two other men were silent, and tried to look defiant as they awaited their turn. The distant sounds of the other man had faded for a few minutes, then there was a sharp shriek in the unmistakable voice of Joel, then silence. The outlaws exchanged nervous glances. Then, without warning, an unearthly racket erupted. There is no such chaos as the sound of a braying donkey, except the sound of a mare donkey separated from her foal, and the shrieking of the foal's reply.

The soldiers returned in the same way they departed, following the Gypsy Queen. Only this time they were dragging a belligerent donkey colt. The colt was tied to the tree that the man had been taken from, and the braying back and forth was furious. The Gypsy Queen chanted, "Forever separated, yet always as one." She waved the smoking censer, and turned to look at the other two outlaws. They were clearly in shock.

Peter squirmed frantically to get free from his bonds, and Matson wet his pants as he was on the verge of tears.

The Gypsy Queen continued to move toward the men, but Cornelius intervened. "That's enough magic for one day, old woman," he commanded. "Your people can eat that one tonight."

The Gypsy Queen looked irritated like she had been deprived of some great pleasure. She was actually surprised at the captain's play. She had not considered him capable of it. *Well done, Cornelius*, she thought, *well done.*

Captain Cornelius rubbed his hands together and muttered, "Let's see if these boys have found their voices."

"The princess and the man got away!" Matson cried out. He had to yell over the noise of the braying donkey colt. "We don't even know where they are!" The ploy had worked on his mind nicely.

Peter joined in the confession party when the captain looked him in the eyes. "It's true. And Rhenska, the witch, murdered our leader." The lad looked pathetic with one side of his face swelling up and the other side burned.

In the background, the Gypsy Queen patted the donkey as she consoled, "Joel, Joel, your flesh will sustain us. It is a noble fate."

"Who was your leader?" Captain Cornelius asked briskly.

Peter hesitated only long enough for the captain to glance over at the Gypsy Queen. "Captain Jarell, he was. We thought he was untouchable."

Cornelius furrowed his brow. "Captain Jarell? A soldier? Were you hired to this deed by a lord or king?"

Peter and Matson exchanged confused glances. "No-o-o?" Peter's drawn out answer revealed their confusion.

The captain's mind furtively searched for any possible motive a neighboring kingdom would have to mount such an attack. He came up blank. He paced slowly as his imagination involuntarily raced through the treason of Lord Darrin from so many years in the past. "Who did Captain Jarell work for?"

"Nobody. He's a famous outlaw all on his own," Peter blurted, then amended, "Least ways, he was."

Prince Lohman interjected, "Was that Jarell, the Butcher?"

The two outlaws exchanged uncertain glances. Cornelius asked, "Did he have a skin mark on his right arm like a sword dripping blood?"

They both nodded.

"And he's dead?" the captain asked.

Again they both nodded.

"Well, that's a good thing," the captain said with a little relief.

Lohman nodded assent, then asked, "Who is it that killed him?"

Peter found his voice first, "Rhenska ... used witchcraft. She has a fire staff ... I've seen her burn great holes through men ..."

The prince and the captain exchanged glances. Cornelius mused aloud, "An arquebus?"

"Must be," the prince replied with a shrug.

The outlaws were baffled by their apparent lack of concern. Cornelius ordered, "Scribe, record the name and full description of every member of those outlaw gangs."

Matson glanced at Peter and whispered, "Don't give 'em any names."

In the distance, the Gypsy Queen was dragging the noisy colt away as an elderly man followed expectantly with an exposed knife. Captain Cornelius pointed at the spectacle and ordered, "Sergeant, don't let her curse or eat any more of my prisoners as long as they comply with the interrogation."

"Yes, Captain," was the reply.

In near panic, Matson called out, "There's five bowmen. All in Jarell's gang. Francis is the best in the land, from Italy. Dark, wavy hair about to his shoulders. Skinny guy. Then there's ..."

"Hold on, hold on, I've got to sharpen my quill," the scribe ordered as he prepared to record the men's descriptions.

Sacrifice

Katrina coaxed Levi to take every step. It was a slow and tedious movement, and his breath was labored. She knew his strength was failing, but she refused to give up on him. As they had crept down the valley, the sounds of the waterfall had become more overwhelming. It was out of sight, but Katrina knew when they were directly over the falls by the rush of cold, damp air that rose up through the foliage.

After what seemed an interminable struggle, they made it far enough past the falls to hear each other speak. Levi insisted, "Go on. I'll catch up later. I need to rest."

He was delirious, she knew. They were beside an open cliff that dropped away to the river below. And a little bit of the waterfall along with the far side of the river had come into view. The treetops on the opposite side were bathed in a glorious sunset. It was a spectacular place where, under most other circumstances, it would have been a moment of deep reverie.

Katrina looked down the trail. It disappeared into a turn about a hundred paces away. She knew it would take them a quarter hour to get that far at the pace Levi was traveling.

"Come on, let's make it around one more curve before darkness," she encouraged. "You can do this."

They plodded heavily for a few more yards before Levi collapsed. Katrina propped him up against the embankment and whispered, "I'll get you some cold water, Levi. You just wait here a few minutes."

Levi, of course, did not reply. Katrina knelt beside her cousin with his limp hand in hers. She mused, *All this water and I have no idea how to get to it.* She did not want to leave Levi, because she feared her voice was all that was keeping him alive. But, with resignation, she stood and turned, and as she did so, was incomprehensibly yanked by the chain shackled to her arm. Before she could register what was happening,

Lou, the big man, scooped her up and tossed her over his shoulder.

Katrina let out a scream that would have put most men to flight, but Lou did not flinch. "Rhenska will be glad to see you," was all he said.

Kartina sank her teeth into his shoulder, and the big man yanked her to the ground. "Listen, little girl," his deep voice boomed, "I only have to give you to Rhenska alive, not with all your teeth and fingers. If you give me any more trouble, I'll snap every tooth outta your head."

Her vision was blurred by tears of terror, and she just nodded her head. The big hand was reaching to grab her again when a large branch cracked across Lou's head. The hit was hard, and the big man went down and dropped Katrina's chain. She bolted down the trail and stumbled immediately over Levi. In his delirium, he barely stirred.

The branch struck down on Lou again, and Katrina leapt to her feet, relieved that someone was rescuing her. When she could clear the tears from her eyes enough to see straight, she lost all heart. The man called Dog was beating Lou with a broken branch. The filthy man was cursing profusely as he did so. But Lou was tough, far beyond a few hits from a branch. He rolled out from under the strike zone, and kicked Dog in the knee. Dog went down, and Lou leapt to his feet and kicked Dog in the side of the head. Even over the noise of the waterfall, the impact was loud. As the branch dropped from his limp hands, Dog fell back and did not move.

Katrina got lost in a swirl of colliding terror and dismay as she witnessed the two brutal men fighting. As one horror replaced another, she could neither run nor resist. When the victorious Lou made his way toward her, Katrina fell to the trail weeping. She was bereft of all hope.

"Get up, girl," Lou ordered.

The forlorn princess slowly stood to her feet. She could not bring herself to look at the big man. She would have thrown up had she eaten anything in the prior two days. Katrina dutifully held out her left arm with its shackled chain dangling. A sudden noise caused her to glance up.

In complete confusion, Katrina saw Levi slam against Lou and bite into his arm with such ferocity, it reminded her of a fierce dog she had once seen. Levi was not a large man, and he was all but dead. But somehow, with the last measure of his will, he had attacked the big man.

Lou had not expected the attack, nor such passion in the fight, and in a split second, the two of them teetered over the cliff.

It had happened so quickly that Katrina did not even have time to gasp. She lunged to the precipice, and the view took her breath away. She saw Levi and Lou hit the water far below, and she knew it was the end for her cousin. She backed up to the embankment and slid down into a sitting position. She could not think nor feel anything but the pain of loss. And with face in hands, she wept.

*　　*　　*　　*　　*

Levi felt the big man struggle against him as they fell. He had no plan. He just held fast to Lou's armor. His mind reasoned that if he held on to Lou, that would somehow protect the princess. With that final determination, Levi was remarkably at ease as they fell. It seemed like a long time before they struck the water. It was icy cold.

There is a surreal level of awareness at the border between life and death. In those waning moments, Levi realized he had lost his grip on the big man, but he could tell the armor was taking the man down. The only other sensation he had was relief from the searing pain. It was as if the cold water had finally quenched the burning that had begun in his hand and had spread throughout his body. Levi was at complete peace when he faded out.

123

Lou was a fighter to the end. With great effort he managed to struggle out of his armor. The big man was nearly unconscious when he finally broke the surface. The river had swept him to a gravel bar, and he dragged himself out on his hands and knees. The big outlaw vomited out what seemed like half the river before he could breathe somewhat normally. His head was still numb from the cold water when he sluggishly looked around.

He saw a peasant woman dragging the lifeless body of the Gypsy out onto the gravel bar. She was wet nearly to the waist. While he was still struggling to breathe normally, the woman came to check on him. He knew he was in a vulnerable position, but lacked the energy to move. He did not recognize the woman. Her clothes were tattered and soiled, and the most important thing to Lou was that she was not Rhenska. The woman stopped near him and picked up a large stone and, before Lou had time to wonder any further, he was struck down.

War in the Mind

Samuel was frantic that he could not locate the princess and Levi. He had come to a drop-off in the forest, and searched east and west. It was more of an abrupt ridge that was forested over than a real cliff. But it formed a natural barrier, and he doubted that Levi and Katrina would go into the valley on the other side. Getting down from the ridge seemed risky, and he knew the valley led to a dead end. Samuel did not know that Levi had been wounded and was failing in body and mind.

Shortly before finding the long running ridge, Samuel had encountered another band of the outlaws. They had surprised him as much as he had surprised them. There had been four of them, and they seemed to be searching for tracks in the forest, just as he was. In the instant where everyone was hesitant, Samuel automatically drew an arrow from his quiver into his bow. It was a natural motion, born of thousands of hours of practice.

When they realized his identity, one man drew his sword and another reached for an arrow. But Samuel opted to shoot the man who was about to blow on the signal whistle first. He had intended to shoot the bowman next, but the men panicked and ran in the opposite direction.

That was the third whistleman arrowed, and word somehow traveled fast even in the chaotic melee that day. The gang no longer used their whistles after that. That development kept the outlaws from effectively communicating their locations, but it also inhibited Samuel from knowing the most recent locations of princess sightings.

He had originally been hopeful that he was in the right area since the outlaws were there also. But after a couple of hours searching up and down the ridge, he despaired. The light was fading when he found an arrow seemingly discarded in the woods. When he bent to pick it up, he discovered another one that had been broken in two. They clearly did not match.

Retrieving the arrows for closer examination, he retreated to the western edge of the hill to find better light. The broken arrow was of normal construction, but, to Samuel's surprise, the intact arrow was one of his own. He studied it closely in the last light of the day, and realized the iron tip was badly damaged. Samuel's mind raced through all the information he had. It was maddening that he had lost the princess, and he was haunted by the thought, *Who got one of my arrows and how did they manage to damage it so?*

*　　*　　*　　*　　*

William and Elise had traveled hard during that day. At one point, they had to pass through a marshy area. It was an exasperating moment when they came upon a small herd of wild swine. The pigs had been lounging in shafts of sunlight at the edge of the swamp, and had not scented or heard the hunters. William had pointed them out to Elise, and they had changed their route drastically to avoid stirring the beasts and thus revealing their presence. When they were well away from the area, William made the observation, "This could have been one of the best hunting days of the Jamboree. We could have gotten at least four of them."

Elise nodded knowingly at the irony of the situation. She also understood the gravity of their mission.

They painstakingly made their move higher onto the mountain ridge in hopes of gaining an advantage. Their strategy had been to set up in a location that would give them ready access to most of the main trails. They wanted a visual platform, but no such vantage existed there. They also wanted their position to be high enough that they would travel downhill when the next signal was heard. They reasoned it would be easier to get ahead of the chase rather than continually trying to catch up to it. It had been an excellent plan, except that there were no more whistles.

As the cold of the evening closed in on the father and daughter, Elise interrupted their long silence with a whisper. "Da, what does it mean? The silence? It's been hours since we've heard anything."

William stared into the gathering darkness, pondering a long time before he replied. "I don't know, honey. I think Katrina has not been found." He did not mention the thoughts that haunted his imagination of all the different ways she may have gotten injured or even killed. He did not need to, for Elise had an imagination of her own. "I'll take the first watch," William whispered.

* * * * *

It had been a terrible day in the mind of Francis. He had missed his only shot at the woodsman, and he had gotten lost trying to catch up to the man. Sliding down a hill into stinging nettles had been only mildly irritating initially, but the rash on the side of his neck had gotten worse as he sweated during the day. His frustration fed his fear and, sometime in midafternoon, he had come to the conclusion that the woodsman possessed some magical ability to disappear at will. And as the day drew on, the bowman realized he was going to spend another night in the cold woods. He contemplated making a fire, but the image in his mind of the woodsman appearing and disappearing like a ghost made him decide against it.

As he lay wrapped in his cloak, Francis had the sudden notion that the prince had been captured. His own dishonesty played the game with his mind that a great trunk of gold had been shared by everyone else and he had been sent away to be excluded. Sleep was fleeting for the man with a guilty heart.

127

*   *   *   *   *

For the first time in a long time, Rhenska was worried. She rather fancied herself to be the smartest person she knew. She was generally self-assured and had no doubts about victory. But her foray into the woods had not been a positive experience.

She was accustomed to being surrounded by her gang. They were a banal bunch, in her opinion, but they offered a substantial degree of security. As the day wore on, Rhenska had lost track of most of them.

Not being a hunter, Rhenska had not traveled far from the old farm ruins before she settled into a windfall near a slope. She had carried embers with her, so making a fire had been simple enough. The problem was that she had no one around to gather in enough wood while there was light for the task. What Rhenska missed most was having people to order around. So when several of the men found her, she sent them out into the darkness to bring in a larger supply of firewood.

That night there were only six of her gang at her camp. None of Jarell's gang had showed up. Rhenska worried that the men were plotting a mutiny. She also worried about the absence of Lou. She had always depended on him to be the muscle behind her orders. He had become a sort of personal guard for her, and she felt vulnerable with him gone.

It was an unusual night for Rhenska to lie down without a clear plan for the following day. The best she could come up with was a plan to evade culpability if the princess made it back to the king. She was confident she could play the role of a helpless woman caught up in a man's treachery. She had gotten off with that ploy numerous times before. Mentally she practiced the lines. '*Mercy, Your Highness! I've been saved! Praise be to heaven! These men have ...*' *then I break down into sobs. Then ad-lib after that. It always works.* It irritated her that she was conceding defeat before the end, but she consoled herself that it was not yet over, she was

only preparing for the worst. Rhenska slept
intermittently that night.

Stand Down the Watch

The king had anticipated some news or action so intensely that he was physically exhausted by the time the sun began to set. The entire camp had been on edge all day and, when the sun went behind the hills, Queen Sarah became distraught.

At length, King Lawrence gave the order to stand down the watch, and the battle readiness was abandoned for the night. The horses were unsaddled and brushed, and there was a general mood of disappointment at the anticlimactic ending to the day.

It was no surprise that a rider was spotted and hailed shortly after dark. It was Sean the Gypsy making yet another message delivery. He was quickly ushered into the presence of the king.

The council gathered for the news, and Sean handed the note to King Lawrence. As the king broke the seal, he remembered that he had ordered their correspondences to be written in code.

In their sense of urgency, Captain Roen and the king assisted the scribe with the decoding of the message. The code key had been passed back and forth so much that, in the end, the scribe determined it had only taken twice as long to do his job with the extra help.

The decoded message read,

Your Highness,

We have by good providence captured three fleeing members of the outlaw gang. We have discovered there was an alliance of two gangs assembled for the purpose of kidnapping the prince for ransom.

Their plans have gone greatly astray and there is a strong disunity between the bands.

They have internally suffered mutiny and murder. One of the leaders, known as Rhenska, has murdered the other leader. To the best of our understanding, he was Jarell, known as the Butcher. It seems incomprehensible that a woman could be so powerful as to kill such an accomplished brigand.

They had mistakenly captured the princess, thinking she was a companion to the prince. They have since discovered her true identity. Evidently there is a spy from your castle, whom my prisoners only know as Harold. They had not seen him prior to the night of the fire in the cave they were using as a base. They have not seen him since, and the leaders have ordered him killed for a price.

The princess has escaped and, as far as my prisoners know, eluded recapture thus far. There is a strong sense that the princess or her guard, so they refer to Levi the Gypsy Entertainer, has mystical abilities.

My prisoners have enumerated by name and description an exhaustive listing of the outlaws. There were just over four dozen, and as I was encoding this message another was brought to remembrance by one of the thugs.

The Gypsies have a peculiar, but brilliant, way of gaining the cooperation of the prisoners.

After reading the message aloud, the king reread it several times in silence. There was a protracted pause, then he stood and turned toward the dark mountains. Somberly he addressed the priest. "Father Geoffrey, I have a confession to make. I have been thirsting for revenge so deeply that I have trusted in the strength of my own arms."

There was a long pause and everyone was silent. When the king spoke again, his voice was choked with emotion. He requested, "Please pray for the rescue of my daughter."

*   *   *   *   *

Elise awoke with a start. Her heart was pounding, and her mind raced to recollect all the events of the previous day. A quick glance at the stars told her she had been asleep for about three hours. She had slept hard, but something had caused her to wake up. "Da," she whispered into the darkness. "Da?"

"Up here," came the return whisper.

He was well up into a large pine tree at the edge of the cliff. It had been a painstaking climb by the light of a half moon, but he had made it as far as he trusted the tree to bear his weight. Even in the whispered reply from the treetop, William's voice carried excitement. He hurried down as quietly as possible while his daughter craned her neck to see him.

When William's feet touched the ground, Elise could no longer hold back the questions. "Da, what on earth are you doing? You're going to get yourself killed climbing up trees like that in the dark. Mother would have a fit if she knew. Were you gathering honey, or spying on something?" The girl's curiosity was out of control.

William turned Elise to face out over the southern valley and, in an animated whisper, said, "Sylvia, look at that."

"Da?" Elise wondered if the stress was making her father lose his grip on reality.

"Sorry, I just was excited," William muttered. "Look." He pointed out the various locations as he explained, "That large glow is the fire at the king's camp. The larger of the other fires is most likely the outlaw's main camp. There are three other small fires. I can only assume those are more of the outlaw's camps. You can't see it from down here, but to the northwest there is a really big fire. That would be the Gypsies."

"So, everyone's warm but us?" she queried perplexedly. The tone of her question indicated her complete confusion.

"No. Well, yes, but that's not the point." He paused and asked, "Are you cold in that cloak?"

"I'm fine," she replied. "What does all that mean to us?"

"The outlaws are divided up," euphoria filled William's voice. "That means they don't have Katrina."

"Katrina doesn't have a fire either?" Elise asked rhetorically.

"Hmm, yes. That's so," William replied. His concern was evident in what he did not say.

"Neither does Samuel," she noted.

"He's a woodsman." William's simple observation of fact conveyed the expectation that his men were fully capable of taking care of themselves and maintaining a high degree of invisibility when necessary.

"What if Katrina is not all right?" Elise asked.

William took a long minute to reply, "We didn't come out here to muse about the worst-case scenario. We are here to affect the best outcome we can manage."

They stood staring at the firelight reflecting in the trees. Finally Elise asked, "So what do we do next?"

"For some reason, the king's camp has not moved. But the outlaws are all over. So I think our best next move is to head for the main outlaw camp. They will either lead us to Katrina, or bring her in. Or, if she makes it to the king's camp, we will have our outlaws." William's answer seemed logical. He added, "If there are more signals, we can adjust our plans then."

Nodding in the darkness, Katrina mused aloud, "We should get some rest."

"Yup," was all her father replied.

Villainy at Its Finest

Princess Katrina woke up before there was enough light to move on the precipitous trail. She was shivering uncontrollably from the cold, and her muscles were stiff and aching from the exertion and abuse she had experienced over the prior two days. As she lay there curled up against the embankment, her mind was numb with grief. She tried not to think of the dreadful death Levi had died as she wondered what to do next.

An unearthly noise caused her to start. *What creature could possibly make that kind of noise?* Her imagination frantically tried to sort it out. Fear gripped her throat. She wanted to cry out for help, but she knew there was none to be had.

The noise sounded again. *Is that from the netherworld?* In a panic she sat up. There was just enough light in the sky to see silhouettes, and something was on the trail scant yards from where Katrina was huddled. She held still and watched in terror.

A man stood up, or more like staggered up. He coughed and hacked like he was at the point of death. It was the man called Dog. As the warm morning glow revealed the glory of creation, Katrina realized a nightmare worse than any she could have imagined.

Dog stood bent over for several minutes. He had been unconscious all night and had nearly choked to death on pooled blood in his throat. The side of his head was swollen grotesquely, and most of his face was covered with caked, dried blood. As his breathing became less laborious, the vile outlaw looked around. Katrina knew she only had one chance at escape, and she bolted down the trail.

As she sprinted for all she was worth, Katrina could hear the man's startled curses as he took up the chase. His footsteps were plodding and heavy, but he was not far behind her as she rounded the bend in the trail. The trail narrowed considerably and made an abrupt end at some thick vegetation that clung to the steep cliff.

She never broke stride, but doubled her speed. Katrina knew she had maybe fifty more running strides to get to the brush. She was not sure if it would hold her, but she was sure it would hold her better than it would hold the large man. *Three steps into the brush*, she thought, *three steps in and I can climb where he can't!* Her heart was racing as much from mortal fear as exertion. She wondered if her lungs would burst, but decided that would be better than being captured by the lecherous monster that was pursuing her.

She leapt over a large curved root that protruded across the trail, and was yanked off her feet instantly. The shackle attached to her arm had neatly captured itself in a fork of the root, and arrested the girl with a severe jolt. The flex of the root had prevented Katrina from breaking her arm, but when it sprang back, she was pulled over the edge. Katrina burst into tears as she dangled helplessly over the cliff. Involuntarily, she looked down at the river below. It was almost serene in its beauty as it swirled along on its endless journey. She tried to shake free, but the rough hand of Dog grabbed the chain and dragged her back up to the trail.

He held tight to the chain as a paroxysm of coughing gripped him again. Katrina had no more tears to cry as Dog dragged her back up the trail. She knew she would be handed over to the horrid gang leaders. She also knew she would suffer much before that. The raspy breathing of Dog was filled with evil anticipation. When he finally spoke, it was more like a slurred gurgle. "You're my woman now. Ain't nobody gonna stop me."

They rounded the curve in the trail where it widened out, and the man picked up his pace. Katrina tried to resist, but she was too light a weight to make much difference. When they passed the place where Levi and Lou had gone over the cliff, Katrina feigned a stumble to retrieve the branch that Dog had used to beat Lou. He yanked her by it and grunted knowingly. She could not have wielded it sufficiently, but she was beyond desperate.

After another hundred paces or so, the trail became comfortably wide with some foliage between the trail and the drop off. Dog stopped and forced Katrina up against the side of the sloped embankment and reached for her tunic. The instant he released the chain, she whipped the shackle against his face with all she was worth. The hit was more luck than anything, and the bolt from the shackle caught him directly in the eye.

The man bellowed in pain, and as he recoiled away, Katrina launched past him. He caught her around the waist and forced her to the ground. He put his scarred fist close to her face and half-coughed, half-growled, "If you so much as flinch again, I'll break both of your legs! Git it?"

His breath was violently repulsive, and his fist was nearly as large as her face. Her last shred of hope was displaced by pure fear. Katrina closed her eyes.

Of all the possible next sounds she may have anticipated, the noise that came to her ears was not identifiable. Katrina opened her eyes and, with vision blurred by tears, sweat, and dirt, she saw Dog's eyes roll up into his head. The man went limp, and slumped off to the ground. Katrina wiped her eyes as she struggled to her feet in confusion. A man was there holding the branch that Dog had used on Lou. He looked mortified by something, but Katrina could not understand what at first. Finally the man dropped to his knees and implored, "Your Grace, I am so sorry. I am so sorry. I never thought it would be like this!" His weeping unnerved the girl, and it took her a few moments to realize she was not actually delivered.

"H-Harold?" she stammered. "Why are you trying to kidnap me?"

The man blurted out, "It was never supposed to be like this! He told me it would be a few hours of work and we would be rich. I am a wretched fool! He promised no one would get hurt. He told me they would never know I was there. All I had to do was identify the prince!" The man sobbed as he spoke.

"How did you find me here?" the perplexed Katrina asked.

The man lifted his face off the dirt and looked up at the princess. "I was hiding at the end of the trail. You were running right toward me. I thought you had seen me," Harold replied in wonderment.

"So, you killed this ... man, from your gang, to protect me?" she asked in confusion.

"I'm not even part of the gang. They hired me to identify the prince," Harold began, weeping again as he spoke. "I couldn't let such ... such evil go on."

Dog moaned.

Katrina and Harold looked on aghast as the man began to move. Harold picked up the branch and tentatively moved a step away from the rousing man. Katrina had been stressed far beyond comprehension, and something within her flared up. She snatched Harold's dagger from his belt had plunged it into Dog's chest in one motion. The man wheezed and tried to fight, but Katrina stabbed him again and wallowed the blade around, all the while trying to figure out where his heart was. After several attempts, the man quit thrashing. His head fell back and a trickle of blood dripped from the corner of his mouth.

Katrina stood up shakily, holding the dripping dagger at the ready, but Dog would not move again. "Is he really dead this time?" she asked with a quaver in her voice.

When Harold did not answer, she looked around and discovered him on his hands and knees, throwing up.

*   *   *   *   *

When morning came, Samuel had an epiphany. The night before, he had begun to doubt himself and everything he thought he knew. But with a new day often comes a new beginning.

The cave! he thought. *This must be the arrow that I shot into the cave. Which means that Katrina and Levi came out of the cave where I spent the night. The broken arrow means someone tried to shoot one of them and missed, and they broke it. They must have carried my arrow thinking to use it as a weapon in a pinch. No blood, no pinch. Somehow they must have gone down the slope and escaped that way. No one has seen them, so no one is blowing on their signal whistles. And because the valley has only one exit … they are going to get caught trying to escape the valley. Levi was never really great with directions in the woods. Evidently Katrina is not either.*

Thinking that Princess Katrina and Levi must be in good shape gave Samuel a renewed sense of hope. He decided, even before the sky was alight, that he would rush to the head of the valley and try to intercept the outlaws as they headed into the valley. He hoped that they were not ahead of him. He determined that the time for restraint was past. *Today*, he mused wryly, *today, I am taking their war to them.*

As soon as it was light enough to navigate through the forest, Samuel set off for the head of the valley. A plan in the mind is almost as energizing as a full meal.

*   *   *   *   *

The king's camp came alive in the predictable manner, and the warriors were ready for breakfast before the sun was up. The king's cook was the king's cook for good reasons. The night before he had prepared his staff in anticipation of the soldiers' earlier start.

As each man came to the cook's cart, the cook handed them a large bowl with a battle portion of breakfast. An assistant handed each man a small loaf of bread and a wedge of cheese all wrapped in a cloth. No one asked the question. No one needed to. The instinct was deeply ingrained into the warriors, and they were as ready for action as they had ever been.

By the time the soldiers were finished eating, the sounds of squires preparing horses and armor was enough to wake everyone else. "Lawrence?" Queen Sarah called out. "What is happening?"

139

"Preparations, my dear. We are preparing for the battle," King Lawrence replied as if he were planning a sporting event.

"I'm riding with," she replied.

"Nope. Not this time," he answered in a non-negotiable tone.

"But ... ?" Her words were cut off by his embrace.

"No 'but.' The men will be distracted from their mission by your presence. Their life is protecting me, and you, and our children. With you there, they will feel vulnerable." He paused, then added, "And I will as well."

The argument was ended, and that was that. The king called his men to order and divided them into two groups. The first group he assigned Captain Roen to lead. Then the king addressed that group. "You are to escort the caravan to the Gypsy camp. Sean the Gypsy will be your guide. Half of you will ride out of sight behind the caravan as a surprise to anyone who dares to assail it."

The first group was not particularly thrilled with being a guard company, knowing the other group would be riding out into battle. The king anticipated this sentiment. He continued with his instructions, "Anyone attacking the caravan is to be cut down with extreme prejudice. The only prisoners that may be taken this day are those who approach with empty hands held high. All others are to be immediately struck down."

There was a general stir of expectation, then the king asked, "Is our prisoner still alive?"

Captain Roen answered, "No, Sire, he expired in the night."

The king looked chagrined. "Too bad," he muttered, "too bad. He really should have been hanged." Looking around, the king spotted the priest. "Father Geoffrey, would you see to a proper burial for the deceased?" It was really more of an order than a request, but it was the way things were conducted.

The second group was ordered to armor up, and the camp broke into a scurry of activity. As the king's squire was adjusting the straps and buckles on his breastplate, the king discerned the young man was disturbed by something. King Lawrence asked him, "Leo, I have never seen you so. What is bothering you?"

The young man hung his head and nervously replied, "Your Majesty, I have no doubts about your ability in battle or any judgment of law … but I have a deep fear about this battle. I have seen the demonstration of the arquebus, which you sponsored at the castle last summer. It was both fascinating and horrifying. I have spent many nights designing what I think may be improvements on the awkwardness of the weapon. But just now, I know your enemy possesses such a weapon, and its fearsome ability to penetrate through armor … Sire, I am afraid for your safety."

King Lawrence pondered the young man's words for several moments before he replied. "Your honest concern is well spoken, my young friend. It speaks volumes about your character and fealty. When your day comes, you will make a fine knight." The king let the words sink in before he finished, "There has never been, nor will there ever be, a battle into which mortal man will ride with assurance of the outcome. But we ride for what is right and pure with the best intentions we have, and entrust the results into the hand of God Almighty."

It was midmorning by the time the king and his company rode out of the camp. Expectations were high for everyone but Sarah. She had overheard the exchange between the squire and her husband, and her heart failed within her. One of the roles that is to be exercised by a queen is that she must present a confident posture before all the others in the court, regardless of what she feels.

Queen Sarah mounted her horse with all the dignity that was conferred on her position. When she had taken her position in the lineup, the captain gave the order and the caravan moved out.

*   *   *   *   *

William and Elise had begun to move as soon as it was light. They had not gotten far when they spotted a group of the outlaws running on a trail. It was at least two miles away and only visible because they were so high up on the mountain.

"Ten or eleven of them," William counted.

"I got eleven," Elise confirmed, then asked, "Where are they headed in such a rush?"

William pondered aloud, "That's got to be the direction of the Falls Valley. It's a dead end."

They had determined the day before that Levi and Katrina seemed to be headed for that valley. They had concluded, correctly, that the two fugitives were lost. They both knew that the outlaws rushing to the valley meant they had concluded the same thing.

"They'll be trapped with no way to escape." William voiced the concern that they shared.

"Do we go into the valley?" Elise asked.

"I think if we do, we run the risk of going the wrong way when everyone else is somewhere else. That could waste a lot of time. Also if we encounter them and they have Katrina and Levi, they could shield themselves, and we would be in the same hostage negotiating position we are trying to prevent." William was working through the options out loud.

"If they do capture Katrina and Levi in the valley, they'll have to come out. There are much better places for us to ambush them than in that narrow valley." He was beginning to formulate a plan. "We should head for the top of the valley where the crossroads will give us the most options," William concluded.

Nodding her head, Elise agreed. "Okay, let's go."

They took off as fast as they could run and slid down the mountain. They knew time was critical. William was a strong man who had spent his life walking, running, and climbing in the hills and mountains of the kingdom. His daughter was again surprised by the speed he could move. However, after about a half hour, William called a stop. The difference in age had caught up to him, and Elise had passed him. He had anticipated that, but it still annoyed him. Mostly, however, he wanted to make sure they stayed somewhat together.

While William was catching his breath, they heard a whistle signal. It was distinctly down the dead end valley. The father-daughter duo looked at each other momentarily. "I guess Falls Valley it is," William stated as he pushed himself to his feet. And they ran again.

They were taking a second breather stop along the way when they heard another whistle signal. It was distinctly not in Falls Valley. Elise looked quizzically to her father for the next order. He just shook his head and replied, "I have no idea. But we need to find them."

Once again they raced on down the mountainside. William was about a hundred paces behind when Elise abruptly came out onto a trail. She had stopped to catch her breath and get her bearings when five men ran into view around a bend. They were no more than thirty paces away when they saw her and stopped. There was a palpable moment when no one was sure of what to do.

One of the outlaws asked, "Who is that?"

And another replied, "We better kill her!"

Elise hastily drew an arrow to her cheek. She expected William to emerge onto the scene at any second, but he seemed to be delayed. "Da," she called out softly.

The first of the outlaws drew his sword and charged as the bowman drew an arrow into his bow.

"Right here," William replied. He was mere feet into the brush. His arrow streaked out of the forest and severed the bowstring of the bowman. The man flew back, sporting William's arrow in his head. The arrow of the outlaw fell harmlessly to the ground.

The rushing swordsman fell only a few yards from Elise's feet. Her mind reeled at the speed her father had sent the second arrow. The rest of the gang bolted back around the bend in full retreat. She let out a little gasp.

William asked, "Are you all right?"

She was pale and a little shaken, but Elise replied weakly, "Yeah, I'm okay."

"That was an excellent shot. Get your arrow if it's not stuck," William added.

It was only then that Elise realized she had shot the swordsman. She looked in disbelief at the lifeless man. "He was going to kill me, Da," she muttered.

Glancing at his daughter, William replied, "Yeah, now you know why I'm so worried about you."

"I'll be fine," was all Elise replied.

They did not have much time to reflect on the meaning of any of it as another whistle signal blew. It was almost directly up the opposite hill they had come down. "Where in the world are they going?" William gasped in exasperation.

"That means Katrina and Levi are still on the run. They're not captured," Elise observed.

"Yes, that is good news," William replied. "I just hope I can keep up with all this."

*   *   *   *   *

A glorious daybreak brightens the world for all men. The way it is received depends on the content of a man's heart. Francis woke in a foul mood after a fitful night of suffocating dreams. His mind was consumed with fury over past grievances he held against others. Many of those trespasses were imagined, which is the case in most unforgiving hearts, but they fed his wounded pride, which in turn stoked his anger.

The first thing he concluded was that Jarell had set him up for something. He could not identify what. Francis determined he would kill Jarell and his closest men at the first opportunity. Somehow, in his twisted mind, Francis found comfort in the thought of revenge. *I'm in Rhenska's gang now, you cowardly sap. The next arrow of mine you see will be sunk into your chest!*

With his motivation resolved and his loyalty shift completed, Francis began his search. He had no idea which way to go, so he made his best guess, and headed south and east following the contour of the terrain. In his mind, he was still searching for the prince and the woodsman. He found the old road shortly after he began

144

to travel, and the miles slipped by much more efficiently. As it turned out, he traveled for several hours away from the action.

It was not until the fourth whistle that Francis heard the signal and knew he was far from where he needed to be. His anger rekindled, the bowman furiously debated about what to do. He considered abandoning the whole thing and leaving. He thought he could cut his own swath of fear as a lone highwayman. But deep down he knew being a solo bandit was a quick trip to the gallows. In his depraved mind, he realized he needed to be important to Rhenska. He also remembered the promise of a trunk full of gold.

Francis turned around and retraced his steps back up the ancient road. He was tired and hungry, which demoralized the man even further, so his return pace was much less enthusiastic. Had he continued on down the valley, he would have encountered the king's war party within a couple of hours.

An hour of the mental fatigue eroding his motivation with every plodding step, Francis again had a minor crisis of will. His hunger pangs had all but convinced his mind that he would die at any moment, when a hapless wild sow with a litter crossed the road mere yards in front of the old poacher. His early instinct overruled any thoughts of riches and infamy, and one of the plump piglets following the sow fell to his arrow. It all took less than two heartbeats.

With his morale suddenly rejuvenated, Francis grabbed his prey and rushed off into the forest. The notion of a roasted piglet to stave off his hunger had revolutionized his outlook on life. He cast about for a good place to cook and rest in relative concealment, and in a quarter hour came to a small rocky outcrop with plenty of hardwood deadfalls. He carefully made a fire with dry wood to avoid making a smoke trail. By the time the fire had burned down to embers, the game had been cleaned and was skewered on a stick for roasting.

Francis leaned back against a tree to await his feast. And there he promptly fell asleep.

Averted Coup

At first light, Rhenska summoned in as many men as could be located by the half dozen men in her camp. When they had gathered, she shared the last of the bread and cheese that she had, which encouraged the gang considerably. She began with a rousing call to double their efforts. She shared all the latest information she possessed regarding the location of the princess, which was remarkably accurate. She described her latest plan to trap the girl in the valley and immediately kill the Gypsy. And she finished by repeating the promise of unimaginable riches. She played on the men's fears and illicit desires so effectively that they all were renewed in their crime.

Except one man from Jarell's gang had emboldened himself during the night. When Rhenska ordered the men to rush to the valley, he stood up and shakily demanded, "How do we know you won't kill us the way you did Jarell?"

She briefly considered shooting him with her arquebus, but decided they were short enough on numbers. She quickly searched her memory and recalled the man's name. "You're Darius, right?" she asked.

"Um, yes, ma'am," he replied nervously.

"I've been noticing you and your hard work," she continued. "You are a good man to have in a gang, and you are welcome into mine when this is all over. But there is something you all need to know. Your former leader, Jarell, propositioned me that we should take all the gold. Just the two of us. And turn the king's men on our gangs. And us slip away to southern Spain together. I think he may have had something for me, if you know what I mean." She paused and gave the men a knowing look.

The men that had belonged to Jarell's gang all shifted uncomfortably at the idea that their former leader would double-cross them. Rhenska continued, "I always take care of my men. And I never let a betrayer survive. It's a bad business if you can't trust the people you work with. That is why he had to die."

She directed her attention back to Darius again and, with a sigh, said, "We are going to be fabulously wealthy when this is done. And anyone who works with us will have the opportunity to join my gang. And anyone who betrays us … will be dealt with."

Darius was nodding affirmation even as Rhenska's final words were being spoken. "I would very much like to join your gang when we are done with this job," he eagerly blurted.

There were about thirty of them when they raced up to the mouth of the valley. The original bunch that left Rhenska's camp had met up with another group of five. They hastily passed the word and, as a unified gang, they made their way down the trail. The trail narrowed quickly and the terrain steepened until the men had to walk single file. It did not take long for the gang to get spread out over a fairly long stretch of trail. But their confidence in finding the princess and having her cornered on the trail caused them to press on.

When it became completely obvious that the trail was the only way into and out of the valley, and the river was a long way down, the leading men began to hasten their pace. They still harbored some concern that the Gypsy had some mystical power. Darius was eager to prove his worth to his new master, so he had taken the lead position of the long group. Nervously, he drew his sword as a precaution. He realized he would be the one to encounter the Gypsy first, and he determined that he would strike the man down before he had a chance to ply any dark craft.

The moment of encounter came as Darius turned a bend in the narrow trail. He had so expected to see the Gypsy first that he was momentarily spellbound. He stood rooted for a long ten count as the others crowded up behind him.

"Treachery!" was the first word out of the man's mouth. "Treachery!" Darius repeated, then rushed forward. Someone behind him blew on a whistle.

Cornered

Princess Katrina approached the hostler cautiously. She was terrified in his presence, knowing he had betrayed her to the villains. She held the dagger at the ready position as if it were a rapier. "Harold, what do you want with me?" Her words were a mixture of fear and indignation.

The man never looked up, but pleaded, "My Grace, please slay me now. Otherwise, I will have to face the king's justice, and my family will be humiliated and ruined."

"Justice is critical to maintain order in a society," Katrina replied. She recognized the words as those from her lessons on civic duties. She had never given the concept any further thought beyond reciting the words back to the instructor during her tutoring.

The man let out a little sob as he muttered, "I know, I know. I am a wretch." He stood up and hesitantly made for the cliff.

The girl called out, "Wait! What are you doing?"

"I must," he replied piteously.

The thought of the man jumping to his death before her eyes seemed unbearable in her mind. "Could you help me get back to my father?" she asked. "Maybe he will look on you with some mercy."

The man shook his head knowingly as he replied, "That will not erase my crime. My guilt is on me. And death is my proper reward. It can't be any other way."

She knew he was correct. She somehow felt empathy for the man. He was a betrayer, without a doubt, but his conscience had afflicted his soul to sorrow. His plight was pathetic and his death was assured. A thought occurred to the girl and she urged, "Harold, if you help me escape from these evil men, I will speak to my father on your behalf." She paused for a moment, then finished bluntly, "We both know the price for treason. And I can promise no outcome, but I believe even if the fate is the same, the shame will be expunged. Surely you will be remembered as the one who delivered me safely to my father."

Slowly the man stepped back from the edge of the cliff. His shoulders never came up and his chin remained low. And he could not bring himself to look the princess in the eye. "How can I help you, My Grace?" he asked meekly.

Cautiously she said, "Can you remove this shackle from my arm? It has chafed me to blood."

The hostler tried to remove the lock bolt to no avail. In frustration he muttered, "I'm sorry, My Lady, I need the wrench."

She sighed and wrapped the chain around her arm as she had been doing. "We had best get moving," was all she replied.

As she stepped over the body of Dog, she motioned to the dead man's sword and ordered, "You'd better grab that weapon. We'll most likely need it today."

Harold drew the sword and looked at the poorly-kept blade. He confessed, "I have no idea how to use it."

With the dagger she held, Katrina made an overhand chopping motion. "On their first day of weapons training, they teach the squires to chop like they're cutting wood. 'Strike to the shoulder.' They say that a lot to the new boys. It is supposed to break a man's collarbone so he can't wield a weapon," she explained.

The hostler mimicked the motions. Katrina thought he was a sad substitute for a real soldier, but he was a man with man's arms. Harold asked, "Should I lead or follow you?"

Katrina pondered for a moment, then asked, "Do you know of a good place for us to hide?"

For the first time, the man held his head up with a little hope. He replied, "The outlaws abandoned the cave after the fire. As far as I know, they seem to think it's haunted. We could hide in there."

The princess was not sure, but could come up with no better idea, so she asked, "Can you find the way back?"

"Yes!" he replied hastily. Then, after a slight pause, he amended his claim. "I'm pretty sure I can."

"Then you lead," she replied with a gesture of the knife blade.

They cautiously picked their way back up the narrow trail with the princess following the hostler. The trail became increasingly winding and the vegetation thickened considerably by the time they had traveled an hour. Katrina asked for a break, as she was fatigued and famished. She was not accustomed to going long spells without food, and her reserves were gone. They returned to their slow trek after a few minutes of rest.

They had not traveled much farther when Harold began to examine a section of the hillside. "I'm sure this is where I came down," he muttered as he looked for some seemingly invisible clue.

Katrina stepped back and looked up the steep bank. It was heavily overgrown with underbrush, and a few tenacious trees held on to the impossibly steep bank. It did not seem likely to have a traversable trail. She was about to speak her doubts, when another sound caught her attention. She held still to concentrate and confirmed what she feared. Katrina heard voices. Listening for a few moments longer, she realized there were many voices. Pointing up the trail, the girl opened her mouth to speak, but Harold's words interrupted her.

"There it is!" he exclaimed as he pointed upward.

Katrina was startled, and looked to where he was indicating. About a dozen feet up in a tree was a knapsack. "This is where I climbed down. My knapsack got hung up in the tree," he explained.

She stared for a moment, then urgently whispered, "Harold, a large group of men is coming down the trail!"

He held still, and the look on his face told her Harold heard it too. "Quickly!" he whispered and made a stirrup of his hands.

Without thinking, she stepped into the hostler's hands, and he hoisted the princess high enough to get into the tree. She pulled herself onto the branch and glanced down. Harold took up a pose with the sword at the ready. His form was not particularly menacing, but she had to admire his courage.

Katrina held her arm down enough so that she could wedge her shackled wrist into a fork in the branch. She let the loose end of the chain drop and said, "Psst. Grab the chain."

The startled hostler tucked the sword into his belt. He had to jump to catch the chain, but was able to pull himself up to the branch. He whispered, "Careful. It's really steep when we get past the tree."

Slowly they inched up the tree until they were level with a stony ledge. A harrowing leap from the tree put them safely on the hillside just in time for the first man to round the corner. The fugitives were only barely obscured by the vegetation as they waited breathlessly for one of the outlaws to spot them. One by one, the long, drawn-out procession of outlaws passed no more than a dozen yards beneath their feet. Amazingly, no one looked up.

They waited several minutes after the last straggler of the line had wandered past. Then Harold began the painstaking ascent using the sparse shrubbery as handholds to get them up. It was very slow, and most of the time they were at least partially visible to the trail below. They heard a whistle signal when they were about halfway up and, looking around frantically, Harold hissed, "I think we've been seen!"

They held still long enough to determine that was not the case, and Katrina suggested, "I bet they found the dead guy."

Harold nodded his head in agreement, then continued the climb through the steep brush. "It was a lot easier going down," he remarked ruefully.

*　　*　　*　　*　　*

It had only taken Darius to begin the rush for everyone to draw their weapons and charge behind him. He was nearly bowled over the cliff when he stopped abruptly just short of the body of Dog. Hesitantly he stepped over the gruesome scene, and several of the men gawked at the brutalized body.

Someone muttered, "It's witchcraft, I tell ya. There's no way that puny Gypsy could have beat Dog this bad."

Another man pointed out the carved up chest. "He's cut his heart out!" the man exclaimed.

"That's how they get their powers, you know!" Another shared his wisdom on the subject.

Darius doubtfully pointed out, "I don't think his heart is cut out."

"Check. Pull back the tunic," the nearest man suggested.

Another cautioned, "No! It's cursed, I tell ya, don't look on it, it's cursed!"

Darius inventoried the carnage. He felt no emotion toward the deceased. He had never liked Dog, in fact, he actually hated the man. He had also feared him. It seemed incomprehensible to him that the small Gypsy was capable of such brutality against so formidable an adversary. He turned toward the trail and announced, "I don't know who did this, but we're catching that princess real soon. This trail can't go on much longer."

They had only to travel a few hundred paces before they were at the end of the trail. Darius stood dumbly looking at the undergrowth on the edge of the hillside. It was obvious that whatever trail had been there in ancient times had long since fallen away into the river below. He mused the obvious, "They must have jumped."

The men looked down at the river. "Maybe they could fly after they got Dog's heart," someone offered.

Darius was about to chide the man for his idiotic superstitions, but before he could form a reply, they heard a whistle signal back up the trail they had come down.

"They got past us!" someone shouted.

"That's not possible!" Darius snapped back.

"Well, they ain't here!" came the reply.

And in the opposite order they had arrived, the men raced back up the trail, single file, as fast as they could run.

                    *   *   *   *   *

Harold and Katrina had only climbed a few more minutes when the second whistle sounded. It was almost directly below them. They both looked down to see the gang member with his whistle. He was entirely too fat to attempt the climb. By his general shape, it was obvious why he was so far behind the rest of the group.

Katrina pointed at the man and shouted down to him, "I command you in the name of the king to cease and desist!"

The man stared at her with an amazed look, then he put the whistle to his lips and blew on it again.

"Hurry," Harold urged. The fear in his voice was unmistakable. They were nearly fifty yards above the trail, and almost to the ridgeline, when the stream of outlaws came into view.

There was a general cacophony of voices as the more nimble of the gang members immediately began climbing after the princess. There was a bit of confusion on the ground, and Katrina heard an arrow smack into the hillside right next to her ear. She almost lost her grip at the surprise. Down below, someone screamed at the bowman, "You idiot! Don't shoot the princess! What kind of imbecile are you?"

A fight nearly broke out on the trail before Darius broke them up. He immediately began giving orders, and another fight broke out when one of Rhenska's longtime gang members, Terrence, demanded, "Who put you in charge? You ain't ever been tested by our gang!"

Darius swung a punch at Terrence's face, but he dodged and it was a glancing blow. Terrence went to hit Darius, but he was dragged back from the fight before he made contact, as was Darius. The two men shrugged free from the hands that restrained them. They momentarily squared off, neither wanting to give ground.

"Okay. I think we should split up. Anyone who can climb should go up the trees and chase. The rest will run up the trail and cut back on the road that goes around

153

this mountain." Darius looked at Terrence and added, "What do you think?"

Terrence looked up into the trees. One of the young men who had spent a few years aboard a ship had almost caught up to the fleeing princess. Naturally he had been named Sailor when he became part of Rhenska's gang. His experience in the ratlines was evidenced by his climbing speed. It was also obvious that anyone who could climb was already climbing, and everyone still on the trail was either unfit or too old for the task. "Yeah," he replied. "Yeah, let's go."

With the two de facto leaders at some degree of unity, the remaining gang members raced up the trail.

When Harold dragged himself onto the ridge, he reached his hand down for the princess. He was shocked that the nearest outlaw was so close behind. He hastily pulled the girl up and, grabbing a large stone, hurled it at the man. Harold was not particularly practiced at throwing, and the stone was way too large for accuracy. But, by some good fortune, he hit the man a glancing blow on the shoulder. It slowed down the former sailor just enough to give them a break. It deflected unpredictably and cracked the next man squarely in the head.

The blow to the head knocked the man into a stupor, and his eyes rolled back as he teetered momentarily. His grip relaxed and he slipped backwards. The man crashed through the branches, until one sprang him away from the tree, and he fell to the trail below with a decisive thud. Everyone stopped their ascent and watched helplessly as their comrade fell. Then someone shouted, "They're getting away!" And the climbing was resumed in earnest.

With aching muscles and gasping lungs, Katrina and Harold bolted down the other side of the hill. As they entered a growth of sapling pine trees, the whistle blew again. They knew the outlaws were close behind, or at least the fastest one was. As they thrashed blindly through the thick pines, Harold had an ingenious idea. He pulled them sharply off to the left, and they ran up the hill diagonally backwards from their original path.

When they could run no longer, the two collapsed to the ground.

The ruse worked, and Katrina could hear the pursuers crashing on down the hillside. She looked at Harold, who was wide-eyed with fright. "That worked. That was good," was all she could offer.

Harold blinked and nodded a little as an acknowledgement. They waited a long time before moving. When they finally stood up, Katrina could hardly walk. "I don't think I can make it any further. Haven't eaten in two ... or three days. I've lost track," she whispered as much to herself as Harold.

Harold dug into the knapsack and produced an apple and a half loaf of bread. Katrina took the apple and was about to devour it, when she realized he was probably hungry as well. She pulled the dagger from her belt, but, upon seeing the dried blood from the vile man, could not bring herself to use it on the apple.

"You eat it all," he urged.

"I'll eat half," she insisted. Then, as if the finest royal banquet was set before her, Katrina savored her half of the apple. She was careful not to eat more than her promised portion, even though Harold insisted the whole time she could have the entire thing.

When she gave him the remaining half of the apple, he handed her the bread. It was not like the bread she was accustomed to. Finely ground wheat was a delicacy reserved for nobility and the very wealthy. But, Katrina managed to gnaw away at the coarse, dry bread until she had eaten nearly half. It was made more palatable by the show Harold made when he ate the apple core along with the white flesh of the fruit.

"You eat the core?" she asked in amazement between bites of bread.

He looked up as if he was unsure of how to answer. Finally he managed to reply, "That's the way horses do ... so I do too." He shifted uncomfortably and asked, "Was I supposed to save it for you?"

She shook her head and handed over the remaining portion of the bread. He devoured it voraciously.

The sun was high in the sky when they began again. They were both refreshed and moved quickly, but at a bit of a slower pace than earlier. They came to the old road and cautiously took it up into the hill country toward the old citadel. As it happened, they were not seen.

King-Sized Frustration

The king and his party had ridden into the hill country up the long abandoned road. They had traveled for the morning without seeing or hearing a single thing. The rattling of armor and the sound of horses had drowned out anything else they might have heard.

Near midday, they crossed a point where a small trickle of water kept the road muddy. The water trickled off a slight ledge and pooled, so they took a break to let the horses water. It was a small pool, so they had to wait for their turn to let the horses drink one at a time.

While at the little pool, one of the men spotted something in the brush that looked out of place. Upon closer examination, the soldier called out, "Your Majesty! There's a dead man here!"

The watering was halted immediately to make sure the pool was safe for drinking. Another soldier helped drag the body out for examination. The autopsy was brief. An arrow wound to the center of the man's forehead was pretty easy to diagnose. Once the water was determined to be safe, the horse watering was resumed.

King Lawrence paced back and forth irritably. The king mused aloud, "He looks like a highwayman by his crude attire and utter lack of any trade indicators. He's no blacksmith with those smooth hands. His thumbs have no callouses, he's not a weaver, or carpenter, or an arrowsmith. Too flabby to be a lumberman, and he has no guild insignia on his clothing to indicate any trade. He's far too pale to be a farmer, and he would smell like, well, fish, if he were a fisherman."

The king looked at the men who were surrounding him. "What am I missing? Is this an irrefutable conclusion? Highwayman?" the king asked.

None could produce any argument to the posed evidence. "Then, it is very probable that this man was part of the gang and has, most likely, been killed by Samuel the Woodsman."

One of the soldiers asked, "Sire, is it not also possible that he was killed by Lord William?"

"Very possible, but highly unlikely. When things get ugly, Lord William seems to have an affinity for sticking arrows into the eyes of his quarry," the king replied matter-of-factly.

The soldier blinked at the unexpectedly blunt reply. "Oh," was all he could weakly reply.

Again the king took up his pacing. It was in bad form, he felt. His early training had been to sit and meditate on the facts to solve a problem or riddle. But his complete emotional turmoil prevented him from resorting to sitting. After what seemed like a long time, he looked up and stated, "I would sooner charge into battle with one of the fabled dragons than await a fight from an unknown adversary."

He paced one more step then added, "The suspense is driving me mad. Does anyone have any suggestions?"

There was a long silence before a young soldier signaled he had an idea. When the king recognized the young man, he offered, "Sire, if we spread out until each man can just see the next man, we would be able to cover more than a mile of this road, maybe two miles, as we patrol. It seems likely we are bound to see or hear something along here sooner or later."

The king looked up into the hills. Nodding his head, he replied, "Lacking an actionable plan, that, young man, is a good idea."

At the urging of the sergeant in the group, the king took the mid-position as the rest of his men spread out as the soldier had suggested. They did indeed cover two miles of road. It did not hasten their engagement into battle, but it made them much quieter, which in turn allowed them to hear the sound.

A Wild Guess

William and Elise had been confused by the apparent inconsistency of the whistle signals. They did not know it was even possible that the princess could exit the dead end valley by another way. When they encountered the five outlaws at the old road, they took up the chase, following the three who had returned down the valley.

They had not gotten far when William called a stop. He was not so much winded as confused. He pondered aloud, "We are chasing the oldest and most out-of-shape members of that gang down the valley they were headed out of."

Elise nodded in agreement. "They don't seem to be the best of anything," she noted.

William pointed to the ground and added, "There are a lot of tracks going down into the valley. And about half as many returning. Then there are these three going back down. All the returning tracks seem to be at a dead run."

"Are the other half still down there?" Elise asked.

"Maybe. But why would so many come out at a dead run?" he asked, then went on. "If they were sending a messenger, there would be only one running."

"What if there is another way out of the valley?" Elise proposed.

Studying the tracks, William acquiesced, "As unlikely as it may seem, that is the only conclusion that makes sense."

"Katrina and Levi have gone out the other way?" Elise's statement sounded more like a question.

Nodding, William agreed. "It would seem so."

They said simultaneously, "We're heading the wrong direction."

"So where do we go next?" William asked perplexedly. They both pondered for a few minutes. Then, answering his own question, William responded, "Let's head for the outlaw's main camp."

It was a considerably easier thing to decide than to accomplish on the ground level. Everything was neatly in its place when viewed from the high mountain top, but not so when in the midst of all the hills and forests. They followed the trail as far as the crossing. There they discovered the large company had come from the south, so they were able to backtrack for a long ways. The tracks dissipated rapidly, and William presumed the gang had been directed to disperse through the forest on their way into and out of the camp so as to not give away its location. It was a good trick. But it also meant the camp was nearby.

Elise and William split up by about twenty yards to search more effectively through the dense undergrowth. It took only a short while for them to discover the abandoned camp of the outlaws.

They looked around for any clues they could gather, and Elise animatedly whispered out in alarm, "Da, I think they have Katrina!"

William's blood froze when he heard her words. He rushed to see what his daughter had found, and his fear was confirmed. There was the unmistakably small footprint of a woman. As it turned out, there were several tracks.

"We have to hurry and rescue her!" Elise urged in a frantic whisper.

William stared at the tracks for a long time before he responded. "That boot does not have a riding heel. It has a walking heel." He pondered the anomaly aloud. "Katrina would have been wearing riding boots. They rode for four days to get here."

"Maybe she wore walking boots for their exploration?" Elise countered.

Elise thought her father looked more worried than his conclusion warranted. He asked, "Does she even possess walking boots? I've seen her in those horrid lace-up shoes that women wear in court. And I've seen her in riding boots. And I've seen her with soft boots like the servants wear, when she was off gallivanting about away from her maid. But I've not seen her in walking boots, and these have been worn a lot. The inside of both heels are worn down considerably."

"She's still safe?" the girl asked.

"It's worse. Much worse than I had imagined," William whispered to no one in particular.

He looked at his daughter and, shaking his head, answered the question in her eyes. "I know who their leader is." He paused momentarily. "The 'R' on that ransom note stood for 'Rhenska.' Why didn't I think of that when we saw the note? She's notorious in most of the surrounding kingdoms. Utterly ruthless." William stopped his soliloquy. "We've got to go now," he ordered.

"Where to?" Elise asked.

William's forehead was furrowed as he replied, "We need to find one of those villains and kill him so we can signal with his whistle!"

"Huh? That would call them to us," Elise retorted.

"Exactly!" William called back as he rushed through the woods.

*   *   *   *   *

Samuel was working his way down a ridge when he spotted the man some half mile distant. It was Francis the Bowman trudging down the old road away from the citadel, though Samuel did not know his identity. But the way he carried his longbow made the woodsman presume he was the mysterious bowman who had shot at him. The man had an unmistakable gait which Samuel noted for future reference.

The direction and seeming determination of the mystery bowman stirred many questions in Samuel's mind. He chose to follow along the ridgeline as far as he could go without exposing his location. At length, the bowman continued on until he was out of sight around a long curve.

He was considering what to do next, when the first signal came. It had come from far behind him, and Samuel opted to go where he thought he would find the princess. He despised the idea of losing track of the man who had been hunting him, but he knew his greater duty was to protect the princess at all costs. When he was most of the way to the trailhead, a new signal was sounded on the ridge he had been traveling. *What is happening? I would have been closer if I had remained lying down!* he thought with extreme agitation.

So, reversing direction once again, Samuel headed back up the ridge as he pondered the mysterious location changes of the signals. He mused over the possibilities, and he came to the conclusion that all his options were bad. He realized that it was possible that the outlaws were baiting him into a trap. He also considered that there may have been some hidden entrance to the valley that was being utilized. And it also occurred to him that the outlaws could simply be confused.

Samuel took a breather and pondered the three options. There were no further sounds, and he felt that was even more baffling than before. He made a guess and returned toward the trailhead. He wished he had something better to go on than signals from whistles that belonged to the enemy.

What Samuel did not guess was that the bandits were passing within one hundred yards of where he had turned around when he headed back down to the valley.

Hedging Her Bets

Once she had sent the men off to the valley, Rhenska had decided to move camp again. She had become increasingly nervous about the entire operation. And when she considered that she had not seen Lou for over twenty-four hours, she knew something had gone wrong. She had made her backup plan, and was in the process of making a backup to that plan, when she had the sudden premonition to move.

She traveled about a mile and found a vantage overlooking the old road. She had just settled in for the wait when she heard the whistle blow up the opposite mountain. *Where in the devil are they?* she wondered. *That is on the wrong side of that ridge!*

At that point, Rhenska decided the men were lost and confused. She felt a certain degree of paranoia that she may be the target of some double-cross plan. So she determined to lie low.

It was over an hour later when she saw Terrence and Darius leading about half of the men down the old road. They had all fanned out in a formation of sorts and were clearly searching the hillside for signs. *So they've lost them again!* Rhenska fumed. *And on the wrong side of the mountain!*

Rhenska decided someone needed to die to get her point across effectively. She silently stole to the edge of the brush she had been hiding in. Her mind was sorting through the odd fact that all the youngest and most agile men were missing from the group. She held her arquebus at the ready and sarcastically called out, "Have you boys lost the valley too?"

The men near enough to hear her jumped at her sudden appearance from thin air. Darius spoke first. "M' lady," he called out in surprise. "We had them cornered, but they slipped out of the valley by a secret way."

Terrence, not wanting to appear as a follower, added, "We sent the young fellows up the slope after them. It was a steep climb."

Rhenska was speechless for a moment as she tried to decide who to kill. Suddenly one of the men let out a yell, and almost immediately afterwards, the sounds of the rest of the gang thrashing down the hillside was heard.

Two men were dragging someone, and a cheer went up from the men on the road. "They've got her!" someone yelled, and a good deal of hooting followed.

However, when the younger set of the gang arrived at the road before Rhenska, they did not have the princess. They had one of their own men. He had collapsed as they ran down the hill and, thinking he would come to, his friends had dragged him down the rest of the way. To their dismay, the man was quite dead, whether from heart attack or some other exertion-related event, they had no clue.

After all the confusion of the men was sorted out, Rhenska asked, "Where is the girl?"

There was a long pause before Sailor spoke, "I saw her with the spy. They were running straight down the hill ... this way. We never let up and we should have gotten them, or they should have fallen into your hands here."

"Yes, indeed you should have caught them," Rhenska sneered. "Where is the Gypsy?"

The men cast about with furtive glances, and Darius finally answered, "We never saw him." He gulped back the urge to tell about the dead man they found.

Terrence jumped on the opportunity to fill in the story. "We found the man they called Dog. He was beat to death pretty bad. And the Gypsy had cut his heart out."

"What? What are you babbling about?" Rhenska snapped. She was not easily unnerved, but that account had addled her.

"They're working in the dark arts," Sailor shakily replied.

Pointing out Darius, Terrence, and Sailor, Rhenska ordered, "You three come up here. The rest of you fan out into groups of five ... " She looked at their reduced numbers, then revised her order, "into groups of four. Search this valley back to the old farm. If you do not find them by the time you get there, search again, and don't stop searching until you have them, or ... until you hear my signal. Then come as fast as you can."

"What is your signal?" one of the men asked.

The smile that crossed her face could only be described as malefic. "You'll know it when you hear it," was her mysterious answer.

The men were dismissed to their task and, even as they were heading up the old road, many of the men began speculating about the signal that would unmistakably be Rhenska. A few of the men argued it would be the arquebus. But most of them disagreed, since that was her way of killing people, not signaling.

When the cackling group had dispersed, Rhenska looked over her three new bodyguards. *A sad replacement for Lou*, she thought, *but they'll have to do.* She knew she could not tell them that they were about to abandon the mission. She didn't really want to abandon it altogether herself. She just wanted to put a degree of separation between herself and the amassed villains so she could be that much farther away from the gallows.

She had dodged the gallows in numerous kingdoms. She had even murdered her way out of a royal prison by pretending to submit to the forced advances of a prison guard. She smiled smugly at the memory.

She had been slated for the gallows in the morning, and the guard presumed his own impunity since he was abusing a woman that would be hanged. He had evidently made it a habit in such circumstances. The man was rudely surprised when she had pierced his heart with his own dagger. He had obviously not been paying attention to her hands while he was attempting his own evil deed.

Again she smiled. That was where she began to carve her trademark "R" in the flesh of her victims. It had been many years past, but that impulsive gesture had catapulted her reputation into legendary status. She relished in her own infamy, but was returned to reality by the gathering of the three men she had called out.

"You boys are coming with me. I've got an idea I know where those two are headed. I just needed to lose that noisy bunch for a while. When in doubt, do exactly as I say. And watch my back. We don't need to lose everything we have worked for because some hotheaded woodsman takes a shot at me."

Whereupon they set off down the old road. They had traveled about an hour when Sailor heard a noise. He had been walking at the point position, and was also the youngest with the most acute hearing. He held up a hand, and they all stopped to listen. "Horse and armor," the younger man whispered.

The men all followed Rhenska as she dodged into the forest. When they were well-concealed by the trees, they waited silently as the clang and rattle of the mounted warrior passed by. Rhenska looked perplexedly at the men. "One?" she whispered rhetorically.

They all shrugged. It did not make much sense to them until they began to head back to the road. Before they got to it, they heard another rider. The outlaws crept back to their safe place and waited again. Again they tried to return to the road, and again they were turned back by the presence of a mounted soldier.

The sound of an order being transferred down a line of soldiers could be heard. Then the sound of the company making an about-face was followed by the soldiers traveling in the reverse direction.

Rhenska cursed quietly. "They're patrolling the road. They've spread out to cover more territory, but remain in sight of each other to assure security." She shook her head slowly. "That means the girl hasn't made it back to the king, so our mission is still good."

Again she slowly shook her head in frustration. "We are so close to that junction with the old river road," she bemoaned.

The men stood in silence for a few minutes as Rhenska pondered their next move. Ultimately, it was Darius who broke the spell. "I smell roasting pork."

It was subtle, but it was true. Sailor perked up and whispered, "Me too. My insides are gnawing at me."

In a moment, they all smelled the tantalizing aroma of roasting pork. Cautiously, they edged their way toward the source. When the cookfire finally came into sight, Rhenska nearly exploded with rage. When Rhenska was enraged, she became sickeningly sweet to her victim.

Rhenska strode up to Francis and, as the man murmured, "Mother," Rhenska poked the barrel of her arquebus against his face.

*　　*　　*　　*　　*

Samuel had been at a place where he could see a long stretch of the road. When the gang had cheered, thinking they had the princess, he took cover and watched from a great distance. He could not hear any of the exchange, but he was astonished to see a woman clearly giving directions. When she had dismissed the gang to head back up the valley, Samuel was again surprised that the leader and three men headed down the valley. They were, he mused, heading the same direction that the bowman, Francis, had traveled.

Samuel made the snap decision to follow the leader and her cadre. He had no clue she was hedging the odds by staging her escape one step at a time.

He hurried to the road and waited until a half hour had passed before he actually slipped onto the road and followed his quarry.

*　　*　　*　　*　　*

Harold heard them first, and pulled Katrina into the brush beside the road. A group of four men went tramping by in a big hurry. It was obviously some of the gang. They even recognized one or two of them. When the men had passed, they silently crept on.

They had numerous other encounters with other small groups like the first. It kept them on edge, but did not keep them from moving. When Katrina and Harold had

167

finally gotten to the old farmyard, there was a gathering of a dozen of the outlaws at one place. The two stayed in the forest as they skirted the farm. Even from that distance, it was evident that the men were disturbed by what they saw.

When at long last they came to the citadel, it was midafternoon. Katrina had the urge to run for the perceived safety of the stone cave, but discretion restrained her. A group of four outlaws came to the well-trampled flat that was before the place. They looked around nervously and hastened on. It was obvious they were not at peace with what had happened in that place.

After a safe amount of time, the two fugitives slipped into the darkness of the cave. They listened for any further sounds of pursuit and, hearing none, Katrina sat down and wept. She had expected to have a sense of invulnerability in the citadel, but all she felt was fear and isolation. Harold stood by, wringing his hands.

Dreaming of Mother

It had been a long time since Francis had dreamed about his mother. She had died when he was young. When his father remarried, his stepmother was less than loving to him. Francis had all but forgotten his childhood, but for some reason, the wafting smell of roasting pig, filtering its way into his senses, caused the bowman's unusual dreams.

He had really not been asleep for long when his dream was interrupted by his mother's voice. "What are you doing, little one?" she was calling. He could even feel her tender kiss on his cheek.

Francis bolted awake suddenly. The kiss on his cheek had turned cold and steely. He opened his eyes to discover that Rhenska was touching his face with the muzzle of her arquebus. Looking up the barrel at the cold-eyed woman put a chill in his heart like he had never experienced before. He gulped.

"What are you doing here, sweetheart?" she demanded softly.

The endearing term was a stark contrast to the barrel of the firearm that was pressed against his face. "Mother! I was dreaming of Mother," his reply was slurred from the grogginess of sleep.

His eyes blinked with a start, then darted around the circle of spectators. "I had to eat. I've been all over looking for the woodsman," Francis replied. It sounded more like a petition than a report. "Have we caught the prince?" he asked in confusion.

There was a protracted pause during which Rhenska realized the bowman had been out for a long time without contact. "There is no prince," she stated flatly. "There is a princess. Have you killed the woodsman?" she demanded.

He shook his head to the negative, expecting to hear the roar of the dreaded weapon.

"How long have you been camped in this place?" she asked as she removed the barrel from his face. She knew she could not fire the weapon without being overrun by the nearby soldiers.

His mind was still foggy from sleep and terror. Shakily he answered, "I, I don't know. I killed this pig while running up the road. I thought it might give me energy to eat. I made the fire and … I guess I've been asleep a half hour or so. The pig is about done."

Rhenska looked around. It was obvious that the man had not been there long. That much he said was true. "What would Captain Jarell say about this?" she pressed.

"I don't know. I've never been hunting someone so hard to find," he replied uncomfortably. "I had hoped to join your gang … actually."

"Good, because Jarell is dead. I killed him as he was trying to double-cross the whole alliance," Rhenska lied casually.

Suddenly Francis got up to his knees and urged, "That woodsman is good! I seen him arrow one of our boys at maybe four hundred paces. He's really good. I took a really long shot at him, but he could have stuck me right there if he saw me."

"Are you afraid?" Rhenska asked.

Francis shook his head, "No! Well, maybe a little," he replied nervously.

Rhenska thought, *I love honest people. They are so easy to manipulate.* She replied, "Good. You will have your chance to kill him soon, I'm sure."

They all gathered around the spit and devoured the pig. It was the first hot food any of them had eaten in days. It was not enough to satiate four hungry people, but it was far better than the dry bread that had run out.

As they ate, Terrence mentioned to Francis, "It's a good omen when you dream of your mother."

Darius looked up from the bone he was picking. "I always heard it's a bad omen," he countered. They both glanced around to see if anyone else had wisdom to add to the conversation. Rhenska just shook her head in disbelief, so the men went back to eating.

When they had picked all the meat off the bones, Terrence asked uncomfortably, "How are we going to get by those soldiers?"

Pondering the possibilities, Rhenska nodded and mused aloud, "I'm working up a plan." She considered playing the helpless woman role only as a last resort. Not because she had any affinity or loyalty to the men, but because it would leave her entirely without a gang. And in her mind, that would not do.

Darius looked around their surroundings with renewed energy after he had eaten. "It's too bad we can't get to the road. I think we're only about a half mile from the cave where the woodsman hid," he said to no one in particular. "We could hide out there."

Rhenska stopped mid-pace and turned slowly to look at Darius. "Is the cave on this side of the road?" she asked.

Nodding assent he replied, "Yes. And not too far off the road either."

Perking up, Francis asked, "Can you lead us there through the woods?"

"I'm not too good with the ways in the forest and all," Darius replied cautiously. "But, I guess if we go along beside the road and keep heading downhill, we should come up to it."

"Will we be exposed to the road at any point along the way?" Rhenska asked abruptly. She had reverted back to her normal manner of questioning.

Shaking his head tentatively, Darius replied, "I don't think so ..."

Rhenska took the moment to refill her ember can with some fresh coals from the fire. Hers had completely died out. "We may need this in that cave," she said casually.

It was only then that Francis realized the wick on her arquebus had not been lit. He swallowed hard recalling the sensation of looking up that barrel. *That means she could not have fired it after all,* he mused. *Unless there is something about it I don't know.* He decided it was not worth taking a chance anyway.

They moved slowly through the woods. Francis led the way, as he was the only accomplished outdoorsman. He motioned for them to step around or over things that would make a sharp noise if broken. And he held up his hand to halt when the noise of the soldiers was too close. He was without a question the most stealthy of the group. That was partly due to his skill, and partly due to his soft-soled hunting boots. But the others attributed it all to skill. He felt as if his value had been restored with Rhenska due to his guiding abilities. He did not comprehend that Rhenska held no value for anyone except herself.

When they made it to the mouth of the cave, the men made ready to attack or defend if the woodsman was there. Francis slipped in with arrow drawn to his cheek. He had a few moments of heart-pounding panic trying to peer into the darkness after being in the bright outdoors. When at last he could see that the cave was unoccupied, he signaled the others to enter.

Rhenska produced a tarred torch from her knapsack and kindled some grass to light it from her embers. The cave lit up around them with a warm glow. In the light, it seemed much less menacing. Looking at the flame on her torch dancing distinctly toward the back of the cave, Rhenska mused, "Boys, I think we've found where that little wench disappeared to."

Cautiously, they edged deeper into the cave. The light revealed handiwork that had lain undisturbed for centuries. There were the occasional broken tools discarded along the way. And the distinctly hand-carved steps where the natural cave was not safely navigable.

It was the kind of place where the flickering shadows conjured all the fears they had ever imagined. The eeriness kept the gang huddled closely together. Each man carried his sword in his hand, except Francis, who held an arrow nocked on the string. Rhenska had lit the wick on her arquebus, and the slow waft of smoke drifting ahead of them beckoned like a ghost.

*　　*　　*　　*　　*

The roasting pig was a dead giveaway. Samuel had lost track of the gang members in his attempt to remain invisible. But the smell of cooking meat gave him the perfect trail to follow. His only challenge came when the king's guards came by in their spread out formation. He briefly considered hailing them, but he knew if he did so, the gang would flee, and he desperately did not want to lose track of them again. When he finally caught up to them, he was rewarded to find his rival bowman with the group.

They were sitting around eating a small pig, and Samuel's stomach reminded him that he had not eaten in a long time. He could not hear them at that distance, but it became apparent that they were aware of the soldiers. They also seemed to be intent on some destination. He guessed correctly that it was the cave.

Samuel kept a safe distance between himself and the outlaws when they began to move. He stayed just out of sight, as he did not want them to be alerted by anything. He followed more by sound than by visually tracking them. And when they entered the cave, he crept up close enough to see, and was not surprised that they lit a torch before they went in.

At that instant, Samuel decided he had to stay close enough to follow in the glow of their torch. He wondered if they had Katrina hidden in a chamber deep in the cave.

When the light moved out of sight around a contour in the cave, Samuel followed. It was amazingly simple to traverse the cave with even the slightest bit of light. The gang moved painfully slowly, which made it easy for the woodsman keep up.

The Signal

When Katrina again took hold of her emotions, she looked up at the pathetic form of Harold. It struck her as odd that no matter the outcome, he would face the death sentence. It was apparent by the look on his face that he was resigned to that fate. Her mind lingered on that chilling fact for a moment. He also seemed to be struggling with something else. *Was he claustrophobic?* she wondered. *Maybe*, she mused, *he was having a struggle with his conscience since this was the location of his treason.* The girl shook the thoughts out of her mind. It did not matter at the moment.

She mustered the courage to look around the cave. It seemed much different with all the old dead vegetation gone. It was dark with everything soot-covered. As her eyes adjusted to the light, she forced herself to walk to the back of the cave. It seemed like a long way.

The column that she had been tethered to with Levi was exactly as she remembered. She became suddenly conscious of the shackle and chain that was chafing her wrist. When she thought about that petrifying moment when Levi severed his thumb, an involuntary sob choked her throat. She caught herself before she looked down. She knew she did not want to see.

She fancied she could hear sounds in the cave at the back, but she knew it was her imagination playing tricks on her mind.

Harold's urgent whisper called her mind back to the moment. "Princess, there is a stairway here. There may be another way out."

The princess opened her mouth to inform him that she already knew there was another way out. But the words stopped before they came to her lips. The hostler was staring intently up into a large cathedral-shaped antechamber.

A thrill of realization swept through the girl's very being. She had the sensation that she was teetering on the brink between the fulfillment of a dream and a hopeless letdown. Ever so slowly, she made her way around the large pillar-like structure in the middle of the cave. The stairs were carved out of the stone. They were just wide enough for one person to climb, and they went up around that great central column into the domed chamber.

Katrina had to stare at all the charred stone for a long moment before her eyes found the inconsistent shape. When she saw it, she could not look away. "It's the bell!" she whispered excitedly.

Perplexed, Harold asked, "Is this some sort of old church?"

The princess never moved her gaze from the bell, but simply replied, "No, it's the old citadel."

He was suddenly concerned that the princess had lost her mind. Dubiously he noted, "My Grace, this is an exciting discovery, but we are hunted by ruthless killers." In a mutter he added, "And kidnappers."

But Katrina had begun climbing the stairs before he was finished. Harold watched with concern as the princess went purposefully to the top of the precarious-looking stairs. "Please come down, My Lady. The floor is stone. It's not safe up there," he urged.

Katrina fumbled around in the ash until her fingers found what she knew would be there. Triumphantly she replied, "There is a legend about this bell."

Out of the dust and ash the princess victoriously raised a mallet. As she stared at it with ceremonial reverence, Harold cried out, "No, My Lady! Don't do it!"

"This bell will summon help if it is rung!" she breathlessly exclaimed. The look in her eyes was that of one who had completely lost all reason.

Harold raised his hand in protest as he called out, "Who will come?"

His words were drowned out by the deep rich voice of the bell. Inside the citadel, the sound was earthshaking. Katrina struck it a second time, and again the note reverberated throughout the citadel with painful volume. As she raised the mallet for the third strike, a ram's horn call was heard. It was known only as the king's note, and all the king's signalmen had their horns

tuned to the same note. In seconds, there were echoes
and reechoes of the king's note in the valley.

"My father!" she cried out through tears as she struck
the bell the third time, "My father will come!"

Harold was dumbstruck as the bell filled his entire
body with sound.

*　　*　　*　　*　　*

Rhenska was electrified by the mournful, rich tone
that suddenly overwhelmed her senses. "What! Is!
That?" she asked even as comprehension struck her.

The men with her were mortified. They circled around
in near panic as the sound resonated within the narrow
walls of the cave.

Realizing that there could only be one origin of the
sound, Rhenska ordered, "Rush! Rush!" And they shed
all caution in their haste to locate the source of the
noise.

Samuel raced along behind them as well. His mind
was reeling with revelation. *So, the bell is real! Princess
Katrina would be the only one likely to find it*!

*　　*　　*　　*　　*

The king's caravan had just arrived at the Gypsy camp
only moments before. Prince Lohman was in the process
of greeting his mother when the deep tone of the bell
echoed up the valley. Everyone held still for several
heartbeats as the reality of what was happening took
hold of their minds. Without hesitation, the prince leapt
up on a Gypsy cart as if to get more range, and he blew
his ram horn in reply to the bell.

Sylvia whispered under her breath, "Katrina's found
the bell."

Captain Cornelius had been consulting Captain Roen
when it all began. "Prince Lohman! What are you
doing?" Captain Cornelius cried out in alarm.

176

The Gypsies all understood the ramification of the bell, but the soldiers only knew what the horn meant. "My sister's at the citadel, and she's rung the bell for help! I've got to go!" he blurted in one breath. "Saddle my horse!" he shouted to his squire.

As the prince's squire rushed to saddle the horse, Queen Sarah and both captains intercepted the prince. Captain Roen was shouting orders to his men, who were already prepared for battle. "Form a battle line, prepare to enter the field. On my mark, be ready!"

"You mustn't go!" Sarah called out to her son through tears. "You need to stay here under the protection of the royal guard!"

Both captains forcefully agreed. Cornelius insisted, "Absolutely, Your Highness! This is a threat to kingdom security, and the heirs to the crown are the direct target! You must stay in the protection of the guard!"

Captain Roen affirmed, "Absolutely!"

Prince Lohman gently embraced his mother's arms and, looking her in the eyes, calmly said, "Tell the captain where he can find the citadel. Or perhaps Marisa could guide them."

Captain Roen and Captain Cornelius stopped and exchanged uncomfortable glances. Lohman's words had been like cold water striking the face. The soldiers could not consent to having a thirteen-year-old girl lead them into battle. Besides the prince, there was no other person to guide them. Cornelius muttered, "Just like his father."

Sarah stood speechlessly riveted with fright. Her mind whirled with dread at the thought of the risk her son was taking. Sylvia gently took her sister's arm and led her out of the way. "This is the part where the boy becomes a man," she whispered.

At that moment, the squire brought the prince's horse. Another assistant had his arms loaded with armor and weapons. They hastily suited up the prince, and he mounted his horse for his first official battle.

As the soldiers rode out of the camp following Prince Lohman, the prince saluted his mother. Queen Sarah stood for all the world to see with all the poise of her office. The tears slipped out of her eyes, but she did not break pose as a respectful tribute to the courage and honor the men were exercising that day.

They did not take the road as most expected, but went directly into the forest on the foot trails. They had foliage and trees to deal with, which slowed the horses considerably, but the reduction in miles was dramatic. It took the better part of an hour, after the bell was rung, to arrive at the scene. They could not know that Katrina did not have that much time.

*   *   *   *   *

William and Elise had again gone up onto one of the higher slopes to get a better perspective view. They were able to catch an occasional glimpse of the outlaws searching the hills in the vicinity of the derelict farm where they had found Jarell's body. They were a good ways off from most of the action, which was a concern.

Being tired, with his patience worn thin, William was getting irritable. "They obviously haven't found her, but why can't we find that woman?" he asked rhetorically. "For that matter, why can't we find Katrina? Or at least Levi? He should be leaving a substantial trail of clues to follow."

Elise was silent. She too was frustrated by the seemingly abrupt vanishing of the outlaw Rhenska. In the back of her mind, she feared that Rhenska had killed Katrina, but she could not identify a good motive to validate that hypothesis, so she kept her fears to herself. All she replied to her father was, "We're obviously missing something important."

They were silent for several more minutes, and William gingerly stood. "I guess we need a different vantage," he remarked. But before he even took a step, the bell was rung.

The father and daughter looked to each other with wonderment. "I never even thought to look up," William mused aloud.

They both immediately knew what it meant. William pointed to a spot they could not see and calmly stated, "A half hour's walk that way." And they ran.

The Wrong Signal

The outlaw gang was scattered about the countryside searching for the princess. They were ill-tempered, as people tend to get when they are tired and looking for something that is not there. They did not know what signal their leader was planning to use to summon them. Rhenska had not told them, because she meant to abandon them to the king's army. It seemed simple enough to her to pick out the cadre and ditch the rest.

When the men heard the bell, one of the outlaws called out, "Rhenska's signal!"

A shout went up for all those in hearing of the man, and they began to rally. When the bell was answered by the king's horn, the men were taken aback. "That's Rhenska's signal!" another man insisted. "She ain't got no bell!"

"She ain't got no trumpet either!" the first man challenged. "I bet she's got a magic bell in her knapsack!" he taunted.

"Maybe she's got a magic trumpet in her knapsack!" the second shouted in anger.

A brief argument ensued, but the second trumpet from the opposite direction settled the dispute. The men all looked around as if they were being ambushed. "That ain't Rhenska ... that's the king's horn," a third man clarified. "I've heard that before!"

The first man called out, "To battle! Rally to Rhenska!" And they ran down the valley toward the sound. They all had a pretty good idea of where the sound was coming from, and others joined them from the various places where they had been searching. The rabble charge was quickly dampened by distance and they took to marching, which quickly degenerated to trudging. They were thirty-five men responding to the wrong signal, but they were going to the right battle.

Promise Fulfilled

The king's response had been immediate. He had heard stories about the citadel and its legendary bell for years. His wife was a hopeless history fanatic, and had exhaustively researched the city and the citadel in the hills. Its connection to her people was significant, and the simple fact that there was a mysterious lost city had captivated her imagination.

In the king's mind, there was no shadow of doubt what the bell was, nor by whom it had been rung. Katrina had inherited every bit of her mother's imagination, and was known to wander off on random exploratory adventures.

His immediate response on the horn was followed in short order by the soldiers. The order was shouted to charge toward the sound, and immediately the soldiers that comprised the royal guard were on their way.

The guard sergeant had been a guard since Katrina was a small child. He, too, had heard all the stories that the queen had told to her children. Providentially, he was on the farthest point of that patrol when the bell tolled its sound. Without responding or thinking twice, the sergeant dug his heels into the great war horse's flanks and raced toward the sound. His horse was an extraordinarily fast animal, and the four miles that separated them dissolved quickly.

The road led to the citadel, and the horse followed the natural path. The rider and horse were primed for battle, and were confused to find no one in sight as they came into the beaten down area in front of the citadel.

The sergeant did not know the place, but there was no way to miss the soot marks that emanated from the cave entrance. He reined his horse in a circle as the wild-eyed beast looked for the action. There was a momentary pause, then a cry from the cave entrance grabbed the soldier's attention.

*   *   *   *   *

When Katrina heard the king's horn, she bolted down the narrow stairs and made for the door of the citadel. Before she got out, Harold stopped her and cried, "My Lady, it is much safer for you to wait in here! If the outlaws come to the sound, I'll hold the door as long as I can." It was obvious he was petrified, but his strategy seemed to be the best option.

She nodded assent. Her mind was whirling and she simply replied, "Right. Yes." Looking up at the bell again, she mused aloud, "Should I keep ringing it?"

They heard more horn blasts in the distance. Inside the citadel, they could not tell that the sounds were coming from the opposite direction. Harold shrugged his shoulders. "I think they're on the way."

There was a pause, and Katrina heard only her heart. It was beating fast. *Too fast*, she thought. The beats never slowed down but actually became louder. She was alarmed, and about to ask Harold if he could hear it, when he looked up in stark horror.

Katrina realized instantly that it was footsteps she had been hearing. In the back of the cave, the sound of running footfalls were echoing. The flicker of the torch lit the backside of the cave, and the princess had a brief fancy that it would be her father's guards. She opened her mouth to call out, but only a scream came out. The four men with Rhenska were obviously not king's men.

Harold thrust Katrina behind himself, and took up the battle-ready stance that the girl had taught him earlier that day. His action was courageous beyond hope and he was visibly trembling.

Francis drew an arrow into his bow, but Rhenska stopped him with a rebuke, "Don't hurt the girl, you idiot!"

Terrence and Darius advanced tentatively toward Harold. They did not know he was completely clueless of the ways of battle. Harold and Katrina edged toward the doorway.

"Run," Harold hissed.

Katrina touched his shoulder and whispered, "You've done well." She knew he could not last more than a few minutes. As she got to the entrance, Harold struck at one of the outlaws. The man dodged aside and, in an odd turn of circumstances, the last thing she saw was a sword crashing down on the hopeless hostler. With an involuntary shriek, Katrina bolted out of the citadel.

The horse is an astute animal, and the sergeant's horse was no exception. It sensed the danger and, before the soldier could rein him around, the horse charged toward Katrina. The sergeant was baffled by the waif that emerged from where he was expecting to see the princess. She was wearing tattered boy's clothing, was covered head to toe in soot and dirt, and wore a manacle on one hand with the chain trailing behind her as she sprinted out the doorway. His blood nearly curdled when he heard her call out his name, "Sergeant Eric!"

"Double mount!" the man commanded, and his horse cut sharply and skidded into position for the man to pull the girl up to mount. Sergeant Eric hooked his knee on the saddle tree and leaned down. In one smooth movement, he swept the girl up behind him. The shackle rattled noisily against his iron breast plate in the process.

Before he could give the horse the command to return, another shriek was heard from the opening to the citadel. The horse automatically turned to meet any threat, and a woman came rushing out, calling, "Help, king's man! Help me! These evil men have held this girl and me for days!" Whereupon the woman collapsed before the horse and began to weep.

Katrina could not see what was happening, but she knew Rhenska was up to some devilry. The sergeant was confused. He could tell something was amiss, so he demanded, "What cause do you have to petition the Crown?"

"Please! My lord, please! I've given my life for this child, don't leave me in the hands of these vile men!" She wept out the words.

Katrina tried to scream out, but only a weak, "No," emitted.

The conflicted soldier called out, "Stand down, wench! The king will sort this ..."

His words were cut short by the roar of the arquebus. Katrina's mind froze with dread as the ominous sound of the ball tearing through the armor was punctuated with the sergeant's flinch. He went limp and, with Katrina desperately holding on, he fell to the ground with a mighty crash.

In a flash, Rhenska snatched the loose end of the shackle and hissed, "You and me are going for a little horse ride, girly!"

The horse kept circling its owner, but it would not stand still for Rhenska to catch it. The men were about to exit the cave when an arrow slammed into the back of Terrence's head. With a shout, the other three outlaws lunged through the doorway.

Rhenska snapped, "Sailor, hold this chain! Slap her if she does anything stupid." Then for the first time, Rhenska loaded the weapon in public. Sailor saw some of it, but he was nervously watching the cave entrance. Darius and Francis were on each side of the entrance with sword and arrow ready. Francis called in, "I'm going to kill you, woodsman! You can maybe get out far enough to get one of us, but you can't arrow us all at once! You're going to die today! How does that feel?"

There was no sound, for Samuel knew he could not get out of the door and survive against the four. He had not seen the arquebus, but he had heard it loud and clear. He desperately searched his mind for a plan.

When Rhenska had reloaded the weapon, she patted the girl on the head and remarked, "This one is for your daddy if he doesn't play along nice." Then taking the shackle, she ordered Sailor, "Fetch me that horse."

The young outlaw reached for the trailing reins of the beast, but one does not just catch up the reins of someone else's war horse. The animal was trained to protect his rider from all threats and, in a flash, the wild-eyed horse spun and kicked Sailor in the chest. It was not a scared kick, but was a battle kick, and the man was dead before he landed.

Rhenska stared in disbelief at the scene. She dragged the resistant princess farther away at an oblique angle from the entrance to the cave. She had always been quick to formulate plans. "Darius, come here and take the arquebus," she ordered urgently.

The man backed away from the entrance, then sprinted to his leader. He sheathed his sword and took the cumbersome firearm. "Move ten paces away from me and train the weapon on the entrance to the cave." He moved the ten paces, which put him close to the face of the hillside. He realized the strategy was brilliant. If the woodsman was to exit, he would have to turn completely sideways to take a shot. It was a mere twenty paces, and the arquebus was very deadly at that range. Darius felt his mouth go dry, but he nodded.

Rhenska wrapped the chain around Katrina's back so that her right arm was secured as she held the girl close. "You make very effective armor, dear," the woman said as if complimenting someone's cooking. Rhenska produced a wicked-looking dagger, which she held against the girl's throat.

Even as she began her next order, the king and his men came riding over the hill. Without so much as a stutter, Rhenska ordered, "Francis, come ten paces away from me on the other side, and train your arrow on the girl. If anything happens to me, immediately arrow her in the chest."

Francis quickly moved into position. He had grasped the strategy as well. Rhenska called out, "Woodsman, if anything goes funny here, the princess gets her throat slit or she gets arrowed in the chest. Step out of that entrance and you get your head blown to pieces. It's your move now."

Samuel had heard everything. He knew it was beyond hope, but he called out, "Release the princess immediately!"

Rhenska genuinely laughed. "Oh! But dear, you don't have much imagination, do you?" she chortled.

As the king's men approached, it was clear that the situation was bad, and the king signaled his men to stay back as he rode forward to within thirty paces. He was visibly shaken by the condition of his daughter.

As he approached, Rhenska ordered, "Darius, train the weapon on the center of the king's chest. If anything happens suddenly, squeeze the lever."

Darius turned the arquebus on the king. Samuel slowly stepped out of the cave and said, "Darius, what about me?"

Darius did not move, and Rhenska called out, "Greetings, King Lawrence. Welcome to our standoff. As you can see, if anything happens here, you die and this precious little girl dies. Now if you would be so cooperative as to take your annoying woodsman and send back a trunk full of gold, everyone can go home alive."

King Lawrence was mortified that his daughter was at the point of death. He wanted to negotiate, but all words failed him. The tension was palpable, as the standoff had no apparent resolution. The king was on the verge of capitulating when Samuel turned his arrow on Rhenska, "I'll put this arrow in your eye, you witch!" he snapped. It was a dramatic deviation from his character.

Rhenska sighed, "You'd arrow a girl?"

Samuel's resolve flickered, and he turned his aim to Francis. In that instant, he saw what no one else could see. "Francis, are *you* really going to arrow a little girl?"

Francis blinked, but his aim stayed the same. "Right eye or left eye, Francis?" Samuel taunted. "You call it."

The bowman wavered for a second, his eyes averting from his aim to see that Samuel was indeed in full draw aiming at his eye. The image of that four hundred pace kill flashed through his mind. Samuel saw the conflict on Francis' face and called him out one more time, "Are you gonna arrow a little girl?" As Francis began to shift his aim toward the woodsman, Samuel inexplicably paused.

There was an instant of total silence, then pandemonium broke out. Rhenska opened her mouth to order Francis back on target, but an arrow slammed into the side of her head before she made a noise. Almost simultaneously, an arrow crunched into the eye of Darius, and the arquebus fired harmlessly into the dirt. Samuel released his arrow and saw it strike Francis

in the right eye even as a sharp pain tore up his left
arm.

*   *   *   *   *

Elise had never seen her father waver before. He had
drawn an arrow on Rhenska, but could not seem to
bring himself to arrow a woman. Realizing his conflict,
she drew on the woman. When William shifted his aim to
the man holding the arquebus, Elise had the bitter
epiphany that she would be the one who made the first
shot.

Samuel had spotted them, they knew. His play was
brilliant and, as the outlaw moved his aim away from
Katrina, Elise released her arrow. It was a perfect shot.
She knew that when the string left her fingers. She also
knew that Samuel had bargained his life for that of the
king and princess. Elise drew a second arrow from her
quiver, and sensed as much as saw that her father had
his second arrow already drawn.

He is fast! she thought, S*o incredibly fast!*

Too Much

The air seemed to go suddenly thick with arrows. Katrina flinched as the sound of arrows striking flesh was all around her. She had expected to be shot, but had lost track of everything. The princess felt herself fainting, and heard her father's voice call her name.

When she came to, Katrina was in the protective embrace of her father. She tried to tell him everything, but mumbled sobs were about all that could be made of her words.

As she looked around, Princess Katrina had a moment of ethereal realization that the nightmare had finally ended. She saw William retrieving an arrow from a dead man, and Samuel on his knees grasping his left arm which was covered with blood. She heard her cousin Elise say to the body of Rhenska, "Nobody holds a knife to my cousin's throat!" as she yanked the arrow out of the dead outlaw's head. At that point the princess fainted again.

When she came to the second time, mounted soldiers had encircled them in a defensive formation. Elise was gently wiping the soot from Katrina's face with a damp cloth, and nearby William was binding Samuel's arm. And just like that, her senses all returned. The princess wrapped her arms around her father's neck and wept.

It was only a minute or two until the hordes of Rhenska's gang came rushing over the hill. William looked up and muttered, "They've got to be stupid!"

King Lawrence did not get off his knees, but ordered, "Harris, Thom, Fredrick, Charles, Thomas the Second, attack with extreme prejudice! Take no prisoners!"

The soldiers streaked off to do battle with the thirty-five outlaws. A mounted soldier was considered equal to ten foot soldiers, but the outlaws were no soldiers. The battle lasted only minutes, and only half of the outlaws made it into the forest. The rest fell.

As the escaping outlaws ran for their lives, they came face to face with Prince Lohman and his company. Some made the foolish attempt to stand and fight, but were cut down. About a dozen bolted deeper into the wild woods. The soldiers made the chase through the thick forest and took down eight more. But the remainder either hid well or fled where the horses could not go.

At length, Prince Lohman called the soldiers to order and rode for the citadel. They had expected to find a pitched battle in progress. So they were decidedly surprised to find they had missed the greatest part of the action.

As stories were exchanged, Elise had been busy washing Katrina. When she got to her arms, she called out, "Uncle? Can we have a wrench to unfasten this dreadful shackle?"

The soldiers in the vicinity all stopped in shock. Elise, realizing her public faux pas, corrected, "Your Majesty, does any one of your men have a wrench to remove these dreadful shackles?"

Everyone held very still as the king stood and slowly held out his hand to Elise. He pulled her to her feet and, with a hug, declared, "My niece, you may publicly call me 'Uncle' anytime you wish." He knelt back beside Katrina and added, "And, yes, all of my men carry shackles and a wrench in their saddlebags."

The king looked up at his soldiers and ordered, "Someone get your wrench and remove this shackle."

There was a general stir and, after a few minutes filled with a lot of whispering, one of the men replied, "Your Majesty, when you commanded us that we would be taking no prisoners and that we would travel in battle trim, we all removed the tools and shackles from our kits."

Determined, the king grasped the bolt that held the shackle clasped. His hands were strong, but try as he might, they were not strong enough.

When Captain Roen and Prince Lohman rushed into the scene, the chaos quickened. The king asked Captain Roen if any of his men had their tools in their kit. The result was the same. They had been following orders to be prepared to fight without restraint. As it turned out, the men did not even have shovels to bury the dead.

The problem was solved when Prince Lohman heard the situation. His full kit was in his saddlebags. He returned in a moment with a wrench and, by good fortune, it was the right size. As he knelt by his sister to unlock her shackle he said, "Hey, you're wearing my clothes."

She did not even reply. She saw the tears streaming from the corner of his eyes and knew they would just embarrass themselves if any more was said.

When the shackle fell to the ground, a great cheer went up among the soldiers.

Damsel in Distress

Within minutes of the princess's liberation, King Lawrence, Lord William, Captain Roen, and Prince Lohman conferred on capturing the remaining outlaws. A thorough head count of those missing was impossible, but when they did a quick comparison of their respective encounters, they came up with an estimate of nine gang members at large.

A plan was being formulated when Elise called out, "This man is still alive!" A general scurry took place as Sergeant Eric, who had been shot by Rhenska, was given treatment. His armor was removed and a large wound was revealed in the side of his chest. It looked grim to all who stood by, but the king declared that they would make every effort to save the man. A travois was hastily fashioned, and half of the soldiers were assigned to accompany the princess and the wounded man to the Gypsy camp.

There was a brief argument with Samuel, who insisted he would be fine. Ultimately, the king had to order him to return to the camp with the others. When the king looked at Elise with the intent to include her in the returning group, she was ready for him. Holding up a whistle taken from one of the deceased outlaws, she stated, "Father and I have already got this one planned out. I'll blow their call while making myself look vulnerable. When the gang members arrive, we'll take them easily."

The king was flummoxed only briefly before he recovered and hesitantly said, "I had intended for you to return with the first group."

Taking his muscular arm in one hand and patting it with her other, Elise gave the king a very feminine smile and replied, "Uncle, you hardly look vulnerable. That's like baiting a mousetrap with a cat."

The soldiers all laughed briefly until the king cleared his throat to make his next argument. But Elise beat him to the punch again. As casually as if she were discussing a sunset, she speculated, "I suppose your men could shackle me to keep me from slipping away from the group?"

William mused, "Like I've said, 'Just like her mother.'"

Elise never broke eye contact with the king as she replied, "But Father, it's your position that I will have to fulfill some day. I really should be fully trained."

One of the soldiers burst into laughter until Elise met his gaze. The man all but choked on his own breath. Turning red, he apologized, "Sorry, m' lady."

Finally the king replied, "Do you practice this kind of banter when you are ghosting about in the forest? What is it with the women in this family? You're hardly vulnerable yourself!"

"So we're going with that plan?" Elise excitedly interjected.

King Lawrence looked to Lord William. He did not know if he should laugh, cry, or plead. William shrugged his shoulders and offered, "We actually were going to execute that plan with just the two of us."

"You people really don't have any fear, do you?" the king asked rhetorically.

Again William shrugged as he replied, "Oh, we have plenty of arrows."

*   *   *   *   *

The plan worked remarkably well. They set up at the old farmyard where the outlaws had made their last official camp and waited until it was just getting dusk. Elise had made a fire and was cooking everything the soldiers had that might smell enticing. When the appointed shadows were observed, she blew a few short calls on the whistle.

The outlaws came like moths to a flame and, before Elise could pull her bow up from the grass, the king's soldiers rushed. There was a brief skirmish in which five of the outlaws fell mortally wounded. Those expired on the scene, and three others surrendered and were brought before the king. By the fading daylight, the king interrogated the men and checked off the names from his list of all that were known to have died. They all knew their fate and, before it was totally dark, their final justice was administered.

It was a somber return to the Gypsy camp that night. They all felt as if they had left unfinished business all over the forest. None of the outlaws had been buried, as the king's men had no shovels. And the lingering doubts that are generated when a list is incomplete are exaggerated in the darkness.

By the time they reached the Gypsy camp, it was late. All business was postponed until the morning and, for the first time in days, King Lawrence and Queen Sarah were able to sleep soundly. All the guard posts were maintained, even though any kind of attack on that camp would have essentially been suicidal.

*　　*　　*　　*　　*

With the sun rises new hope and, even though there was a cloud cover, everyone's spirits were dramatically improved. The events of that day were like a blur. Two dozen soldiers were sent out to recover all of the bodies of the outlaws and bury them in the farm field. An equal number of young Gypsy men had signed on to do the digging in order to make some extra money.

As instructed, the position and description of the remains of each outlaw was carefully noted, and their weapons and valuables were brought to the camp. The soldiers had good maps, and it was not long after noon when most of the soldiers returned to the camp. With each report they brought back, names were carefully compared to descriptions and summarily marked off the list. Most of it was predictable with two chilling exceptions.

"What do you mean, 'The body of Rhenska is missing'?" the king asked the soldier in agitation.

The nervous soldier replied, "Sire, there was nary a trace of her where she fell. We looked inside that cave too, but found nothing there either. That's an eerie place."

"She couldn't have survived," King Lawrence mused aloud as he paced slowly. "That's not humanly possible."

The king looked back at the soldier and asked, "So, where did you send the other two men?"

With a deep breath the soldier explained, "There looked to be a few unshod hoof prints. They were too small to be from a war horse. I couldn't tell where they went. So, I took it upon myself to send the men down the trail, the same trail we came up yesterday ... hoping they would be able to pick up the tracks. Did I do wrong?"

"No ... no, I think you did the right thing. I only worry about what they may encounter, being only two of them," the king replied with furrowed brow.

The man stood awaiting the next question when the king turned to the last man to report. At the king's nod, the man reported, "We found the trail that led to the cliff where Her Grace was violently accosted. The first body was apparently the man who fell from the trees. His neck was broken. He's the one missing a finger on his left hand. Then we found the body of the vile one, referred to as Dog. He was easy to identify."

The soldier waited while the scribe marked the names off the list before he continued. "We got close enough to the edge of the cliff to see two bodies on a sand bar. One of them was a pretty big man. I believe he was the one named Lou." The man stopped speaking long enough for the scribe to make his mark.

The king interjected, "The other would be Levi the Entertainer." A wistful look crossed the king's expression, and he spoke in a barely audible tone, "He had written me a letter inviting me to enjoy his shows during the Jamboree. He wanted an audience to interview for the position as court jester." The wistful countenance remained as the king finished his regret, "My steward said he was modest yet very talented. I wish I had taken the time to speak with him when he was at the castle. I just assumed ...”

The soldier waited patiently until the king acknowledged him again. “I sent my men to bury the dead man by the riverside. It looked like it would be a long ride to get around to that side of the river. I also instructed them to bring the body of the Gypsy back here for a proper burial by his people. I know they are planning to have a service for him tonight. The men will probably not make it back by then.” The soldier paused, then added, “If any of my instruction to the men is not in your wishes, I stand ready to return to them in haste and carry out all that you say.”

“You have done well, Sergeant. You are dismissed,” the king answered. Then, turning to the scribe, the king remarked, “By my tally, we are one man shy.”

It was really a question in the form of a statement, and the scribe replied, “You are correct, Sire. I have yet listed the name, or, er, moniker, Porky. Described as being fat, short, mean as a cornered viper, and a cousin to Jarell, their leader.” The scribe looked up and explained, “I'm only reading what the captive described.”

The king nodded. “Quite so,” he replied absently. He snapped for a page, but none had been brought on the trip. Looking around somewhat self-consciously, the king sent a soldier to summon Lord William. In a few minutes, William and both captains were at council with the king.

The king went straight to the point. “We have a development. The body of Rhenska, the notorious outlaw, has gone missing. I have also learned, just now, that there remains yet one outlaw alive from the list. He is purportedly a cousin to the other outlaw, Jarell. His name is Porky.” The king made a face at his own words. As he shook his head slowly, he commented, “What is it with these villains and their strange nicknames?”

Looking up at his council, the king continued, “It seems that this 'Porky' may have spirited the body of Rhenska away. There were some unshod tracks, possibly made by a pony, in the vicinity. Two of our men are currently trying to track them down." The king paused and looked around at his trusted counselors. "Well?"

Captain Cornelius had a furrowed brow as he asked, "What would the cousin of Jarell want with the body of Rhenska? Do you think the division between them was overblown?"

William shook his head to the negative as he replied, "I don't think so. I saw the hole in Jarell. He had been shot in the back with that arquebus at no more than three paces. They surely must have hated one another."

The king nodded, but he was clearly disturbed. "Corpus delicti, in matters of law," he muttered, "in matters of peace of mind, as well, it seems. I should dearly love to know what motivated that man to steal that woman's corpse."

"You shall have your peace of mind, Sire. I'll not rest until my men find the body of that wretched woman," Captain Roen proclaimed. And with that, the king dismissed his men.

In a few minutes, twenty soldiers rode out of the camp in search of the missing outlaw, and with the hope of discovering the motive. Mysterious occurrences tend to catch the attention of many, and it did not take long for rumors to spread throughout the Gypsy camp about the missing corpse.

Almost immediately, stories of witches, wraiths, and other paranormal beings surfaced, and younger children became the desired audience of the older children. It was only a matter of time before the Gypsy Queen sought out the king. She greeted him with a half bow and seated herself on a bench opposite the makeshift table he was working at. He returned the bow as he had been raised to do by Yomahito. She spoke softly, "Dead people stay dead, as a general rule. Your missing witch is likely being carried away for a bounty. I have seen her wanted bills posted to the north and as far west as the kingdom of France. Her evil was known far and wide."

The king stared at the old woman for a long time as his mind raced through a myriad of possibilities. Finally he replied, "You are undoubtedly correct. Though it seems like such a crass action."

She nodded assent and remarked, "Except not so crass by someone who would kidnap a child." They were silent for a moment when a call went up. The soldiers were returning. They had been gone no more than two hours, and they not only had the quite-dead corpse of Rhenska, but they also had the man who had carried it away. Only he was not fat as anticipated.

The man was thin beyond healthy. He had the pale-colored skin that people develop when they are indoors too much of the time. His puffed up eyelids and bloodshot eyes told the rest of his story.

The man was brought before the king, and he dropped to a frightened bow. He was visibly trembling when the guard lifted the wisp of a man to his feet. He stood with mouth agape as he faced the king.

"What dealings have you had with this deceased woman? And why have you taken her body away? And what was your role in her gang?" the king demanded.

The old drunk had clearly not been sober for very long. He shakily replied, "I was sent away by the constable of my village, Pinewood Town. So I took my nag and came into the hills. And I happened upon the scene of a battle, and this woman was dead there. Your Majesty, I swear I didn't have anything to do with her death. But she burnt down the inn I used to stay at with my ..." The man rolled his eyes up to the left as he struggled to recall the relationship. The considerable crowd that had gathered held in perfect silence as the man came to his conclusion and continued, "my uncle's grandson. He got killed by this witch. She had a magic staff. And I took his kid to his other cousin's farm. She seen her pa get blasted. She never spoke a word that whole next day. She may have a spell on her too."

The man interrupted his syncopated story as he seemed to remember something. He produced a folded up wanted poster. "She put this up in the town, as a taunt," the man explained as he held it out for the king. A guard took it and handed it to King Lawrence. The poster had Rhenska's name, a fairly good rendering of her likeness, and description, along with a sizable reward. "Is this the right time to get the reward money?" the old drunk asked.

The king sighed heavily. "No. That reward is good only for the person who killed her, and it is offered by the king of Este. You would have had a pretty foul mess on your hands by the time you got there," he replied. Then, turning to his steward, the king ordered, "Steward, issue this man a beggar's stipend times two, and send him on his way."

After the drunk was gone, and several soldiers were dispatched to bury Rhenska back at the farm with all the other outlaws, the king looked once again to his counselors. "Our remaining villain is still at large."

Captain Cornelius asked, "Should we begin the search this late in the afternoon?"

King Lawrence looked around the camp. It was being converted back into its regular orientation. The Gypsy way of life was far from the orderly disciplines of the military compound it had become. He knew they were preparing to have their service for Levi. The king suddenly wished he and his entire entourage had never come to the Gypsy Jamboree. "No. We'll begin at first light," he replied pensively.

Gypsy Funeral

Everyone dies eventually. That fact has never been in dispute. But the way one anticipates their own mortality tends to affect the way they approach their life. Levi had been generous to the point of being considered reckless. And stories of his life were bandied about like children playing with a ball.

Gypsy funerals were as unstructured as their weddings and other celebrations. The king's priest nearly had a nervous breakdown at their seemingly cavalier attitude toward the departed. Seeing his agitation, Lord William took it upon himself to explain the customs and lack thereof to the distressed priest.

In his explanation to the priest, William acutely recalled that it had been his effort to rescue Levi, as a young child, from a wild boar that precipitated William's own adoption into the band. The poignant memory got to him, and William had to step into the shadows to let his emotions settle before returning to the service.

William passed when someone suggested he share a story. Stammering for the right words, he mumbled, "I'm not a good storyteller like many of you. Remember, I married Gepetka's granddaughter. I don't actually have his blood in me."

The crowd was satisfied, and another person shared his story. After a while, it was time, and the Gypsy Queen asked Katrina to share her story. The forest became very silent as Princess Katrina detailed the events of her ordeal and Levi's selfless sacrifice. In the end, just about every eye was leaking.

Eventually Father Geoffrey was asked to make a prayer of committal for Levi. His earlier consternation at the disorder of their service seemed to vanish as he began his formal prayer, and after his words, "May his soul and the souls of all the faithful departed through the mercy of God rest in peace," there was a long silence.

After the service, such as it was practiced by the Gypsies, King Lawrence asked if he could address the gathering. It was an odd turnabout, but he was determined to not cause the Gypsies any further pain. When the Gypsy Queen gave him the nod, he addressed the assembly. "It was our intention to join you for this annual celebration of which I have heard so much. I am deeply grieved that this grave evil has come here and afflicted you all. And I have no words to describe the great gratitude I have for you all, and especially Levi. He was a man of peace who sought to spread joy and delight wherever he traveled. He lost his life heroically. And while there is nothing I can do to bring him back, I intend to resurrect the old citadel and call it, in his honor, Levi's Citadel. Within the next few years, you should see it transformed."

There was a general din of chaos as the Gypsies all spoke at once. It was a good sound, as the thing pleased the crowd. Finally one of the elders spoke above the noise. "King Lawrence, you are always welcome to our gathering. I propose we have an extra week of Jamboree this year, since we have not actually celebrated yet."

There was hearty concurrence among the cacophony, and The Gypsy Queen declared a full extra week of Jamboree. The mood as the assembly dispersed to their tents was considerably better than when they convened. As Marisa and Katrina approached the princess's tent, a figure loomed in the darkness before them. Before either of the girls could make a sound, Gretta whispered, "Beggin' your pardon, M' Lady, I didn't mean to frighten you."

"Miss Gretta!" Katrina gasped under her breath, "I haven't seen you all day!"

"M' Lady, now that we've laid Levi to rest, I need to tell you where I've been," Gretta whispered urgently. "I only got back into the camp a little while ago. I went searching for you in the forest and I got mighty lost."

The princess touched the maid's arm. "You've been lost in the forest all this time?" she asked in wonder. Then she suddenly withdrew her hand, "You smell ... um, pungent."

"Yes, M' Lady. I'll get a bath before I speak to you again," Gretta replied.

"Okay, you can find me in the tent," the girl responded. "Miss Gretta? Are you alright?"

The maid took a long time to reply. "I've had better times, M' Lady. I've been worried to death for you. I saw you on that cliff on the other side of the river. At least the other side from me. I screamed out as loud as I could to warn you about that nasty-looking man. But I don't think you could hear anything over that waterfall. I've cried about every hour since then 'til now, seein' you all safe here."

Katrina was electrified by Gretta's words. "You saw me on that cliff?!" she gasped.

"Yes, M' Lady," Gretta replied.

Katrina took Gretta's hands and urged, "Promise me, as soon as you have bathed, you will come to my tent and tell me everything that happened since I last saw you."

Gretta promised, but no one draws a bath and lays out clothing for a maid. By the time Gretta was cleaned up and got back to the princess's tent, both girls were sound asleep.

*   *   *   *   *

When Katrina awoke the next morning, she felt confused, but could identify no reason for it. She discovered that Marisa had already gotten up, so she quickly dressed in what Gretta had laid out for her.

There was a large group of soldiers preparing to ride out for what Katrina assumed to be a mission to locate the final outlaw. It seemed, in her mind, that there was a lot of country out there where a man could hide. *Odd,* she thought, *it didn't seem like so much when I was trying to hide.*

She found her maid airing blankets on a line and rushed to her. "Miss Gretta! I want to hear about your

201

adventures from when you were lost," the princess gushed out.

The maid began, "Well, M' Grace. Yesterday about midafternoon ..."

"No, no! Start with the beginning. I want to hear every bit," the princess insisted as she pulled the older woman onto a bench beside her.

Gretta seemed conflicted, but almost reluctantly she began, "After that horrible morning when you and Lady Marisa were missing, I stayed around the captain to learn as much as I could. When Samuel went into the forest, I thought to myself, 'Gretta, if that man can wander around in the forest, you can too. And besides that, you probably can guess where the princess might go better than that woodsman.'

"I was surely wrong. I came to a creek and thought it would be best to follow it downstream. When it came to another creek, I followed that one back up into another valley to get across it where it would be shallow. It was a cold night in the mountains, and I was afraid being all alone. I took up a stout stick in case somebody or something tried to get at me. It was a good thing I loaded up my pockets with bread and cheese.

"The next day I wandered around trying to find a shortcut back, but just got good and lost. I went down the other side of that stream and slid down on a lot of loose stones. When I got stopped, I had almost slid over a steep cliff into the river. It took me a long time to get down by the river without falling. By then I was pretty scared. I hadn't seen you or anyone, and I was afraid they had caught you. I done some cryin' and prayin' down by that river."

The princess interrupted, "Was that near the waterfall?"

"Yes, M' Lady," Gretta replied, "I could hear it, but I couldn't see it. I was over the top of it then. I tried to find a way back up, but couldn't. So I went to the edge of the river and followed it to the falls. It was a powerful noise. I climbed down the rocks beside the falls. It was slick, and I almost lost my grip a time or two."

"Were you afraid?" Katrina asked with newfound respect for the maid. She thought, *This woman has to be nearing thirty!*

Gretta broke stride in her story. Haltingly, she recovered and responded, "Yes, yes. I thought I might die there all alone. But I made it down, somehow. Bless the good Lord for that. It took a long time. It was a cold night down there too. Then when I was crossing a small creek, about knee-deep, something made me look back up on that cliff. It was the other side of the river from where I came down. That's when I saw you and Levi. I was so excited, I shouted for you, but the waterfall was too much. Then I saw that big man come and that other big man, and it was horrible. Then I saw the worst thing in my life when that big man and Levi went off that cliff. It seemed like it took forever for them to hit the water."

"Riders coming in!" The call was shouted so near the princess and Gretta that they both jumped. They had been so engrossed in the story that neither had noticed that the king was standing nearby listening intently. At the call, King Lawrence drew his sword with such intensity that the maid instinctively shielded the princess.

"King's men approaching!" was the next call, and the king sheathed his sword. In the confusion of the next moment or two, Gretta rose and bowed before the king. Too late, King Lawrence motioned her to remain seated. She was rather astonished that she had not heard his approach, and chagrined that she had not made the appropriate obeisance.

Katrina rushed to embrace her father, and before the princess could take Gretta away from the meeting to finish her story, the riders stood ready to report to the king. Gretta stood silently, and when the king acknowledged them, they excitedly made their report.

"When we got to the river bar, Sire, the big man, Lou, was there, dead as dead could be. He'd had his brains bashed out by a good-sized stone. Someone beat him good 'til he was ..." The soldier abruptly ceased his gruesome description of the scene when he realized the princess was present.

"Begging pardon, Your Majesty. This might not be suitable for the princess," the guard all but stammered.

King Lawrence looked at his daughter. Her normally pale skin was ghost white, and the look of mortification on her face was intense. "Honey, maybe you should go to your mother for a few moments," he tenderly urged.

She did not respond at first. Her gaze was locked on Gretta, the maid that had served her hand and foot all her life, the woman who had bathed her forehead when she was ill, and drawn every bath she had ever taken. The revelation was as shocking as it was thrilling. *This is a whole different side of this woman!* she thought.

Without thinking, Katrina had pointed at Gretta. The king followed her gaze and pointing finger. "Yes, that is a good point. Miss Gretta, you may not want to hear this either. Take the princess and be dismissed."

The soldier making the report stared hard at the red-faced maid. Something about her reaction was wrong. He looked at her feet and stared for a moment. *They're about the same size as the tracks*, he thought.

"Was that you, Miss Gretta?" Katrina gasped.

Everyone suddenly stopped, and all eyes turned to the maid. Slowly Gretta replied, "That man came up out of the water with pure evil in his eyes. I said, 'You done the last of your evil deeds, mister! You ain't layin' your hands on M' Lady ever again!' and I beat him with a stone 'til I knew he wasn't going to move again."

There was an icy silence for ten heartbeats. Finally Katrina broke the spell and, rushing to her maid, threw her arms around the woman. She sobbed as the horrors of that day whirled through her memory. Gretta just patted the back of her head and said, "There, there. He's not gonna hurt you or anyone else again."

The soldier making the report finally found his voice and asked, "Did you kill the other one also?"

With a sniff, Katrina interjected, "He was all but dead when he went over the cliff."

"The fat, little one, with the sinister-looking skin markings on his arm?" the soldier asked, because he felt they were not talking about the same person.

Gretta tried to get recognized, but Katrina answered again, "The Gypsy, Levi. The juggler."

"No-o-o, this guy was from the gang," the soldier explained hesitantly.

King Lawrence asked, "Wait. You said there was a short, fat gang member dead down there?"

"Yes, Sire," he sharply replied.

"That's good news. That would be the last of the outlaws accounted for," the king remarked with relief. He called out to a man standing duty, "Call Captain Roen, tell him to stand down the search. The last outlaw has been located."

There was a general flurry of activity as men rushed up and some rushed away. Finally the king ordered the soldier, "Turn the body of Levi over to the Gypsies." To another soldier he ordered, "Sergeant, take your men and stand by to assist the Gypsies to bury their kinsman in whatever manner of help they request."

To the scribe, the king turned and commanded, "This matter is officially closed. Note in the chronicles of the kingdom as such."

The soldier that had been making the original report called out in exasperation, "Sire, we never found the body of the Gypsy."

King Lawrence had, for the first time in a week, felt relief that the ordeal was resolved. And that feeling had lasted less than two heartbeats. With a new mystery looming over his head, the king turned back slowly. He looked old to Katrina, much older than she thought he had ever seemed. "Are these very hills haunted for all times?" he muttered.

This time, Gretta was less patient and she waved her hand vigorously. "Yes?" the king acknowledged.

"Sire! I laid the Gypsy, Levi, to rest last night," she blurted. "I was just trying to tell M' Lady about it when all this business happened."

The king was shocked. "Where have you lain him?" he asked more abruptly than the delicate subject should have been handled.

Suddenly a bloodcurdling scream was heard throughout the camp. It was repeated, and a general din of shrieks followed. There was some unintelligible shouting in the distance, and the soldiers present sprang into action. Drawing arms, they forced a circle around the king and princess within a heartbeat. There was a palpable pause as the tense soldiers searched for the threat.

"That's what I've been tryin' to tell, M' Lord. I laid him to rest in his own tent. He was much better yesterday when we started the trip, but mighty sore and tired when we got here," the maid explained.

Katrina wrested her way out from behind the guard barricade and grabbed her maid and screamed, "You mean Levi is still alive?"

"Yes, M' Lady. I've been tryin' to tell you since last night!" the maid exclaimed in frustration.

"What is all that screaming?" the king demanded as he joined Katrina's side.

Gretta looked around and, with a shrug, replied, "I expect Levi must have got hungry and came out of his tent."

The maid's speculation was correct. Levi had indeed been awakened by the smells of his people's cooking. It was the first day he was able to get up without assistance, but his sudden appearance, the day after his funeral, had addled some of the women by the cookfire.

*　　*　　*　　*　　*

"One more thing, M' Lord," Gretta requested.

The king was teetering between jubilation and insanity, he was sure. Hesitantly he asked, "What may that be?"

The woman sheepishly replied, "Please don't be angry with your servant. I've only been tryin' to make it right. But yesterday Levi walked for a little while, and I knew he would never make it. We should have stayed in that fisherman's goat shed for a few more days. But I hailed a man with a horse, and he carried Levi all the way up here. And I told him he would be paid the day's wages for a horse packer. I know I'm bold for makin' such a claim, but I knew you to be generous to those who help your people."

"You stayed in a goat shed?" the king asked incredulously.

"Yes, M' Lord. The fisherman wouldn't allow us into his cottage on account of Levi bein' a Gypsy. But his wife let us stay in the goat shed while I nursed him back to some health."

"We'll hear more about that later," the king replied in a befuddled tone. "Yes, I'll gladly pay the man for his service. You were not remiss to make that claim."

In a few minutes, the man was brought forth to be paid. He was thin and pale with all-too-familiar puffed up eyelids. The king called the steward, and as he noticed the man, he cried, "You again! I thought you were on your way."

The man nodded. "I was, Your Majesty. This fine lady told me that Gypsy was a friend to your family and you would pay for the pack animal service. I wouldn't have believed her, but for you being up here with the Gypsies and all."

"Well, your little pony is getting his workout these days. I thank you for your service," the king replied a bit less tersely. "Steward, pay this man a day's wages for pack animal service. Actually, pay him double. Then he can be on his way for certain this time."

*   *   *   *   *

Gretta hurriedly led Princess Katrina to Levi. The girl greeted him with copious tears. She went on and on about what a hero he was to her, and how she was thrilled to find he was alive. Levi's smile was halfhearted as he listened to the princess speak. Meanwhile, the Gypsy Queen was dressing his hand with a poultice and wrap.

Gretta asked, "Did I do all right fixin' his hand up?"

"By some great miracle," the Gypsy Queen slowly
replied, "you did not kill him." The old woman never lost
pace as she spoke.

"Well, I done all the best I knew how to do! I didn't see
you out there in that goat shed offerin' to help!" Gretta
snapped at the old woman.

The Gypsy Queen just silently smiled. After some time,
she remarked, "Your care for Levi clearly outperformed
your actual doctoring skills."

When he was able to break away from the ever-
pressing needs of his entourage, the king also spoke at
length to Levi about his bravery and heroic deeds. Levi
was not particularly responsive, so they thought to give
him some time to rest.

Most of that day, Levi sat around somewhat listlessly
and observed the festivities. Though numerous people
attempted to engage him in conversation, Levi remained
uncustomarily succinct in his exchanges.

The remainder of that day was filled with exchanges of
stories and accounts of danger. And by the time the
music and dancing had begun in the evening, Gretta was
the only one who made a point of checking on Levi every
half hour. He was a pathetic sight.

*   *   *   *   *

The feasting was legendary at that Gypsy Jamboree.
Each day a hunting party would bring in some bounty
from the forest or marsh. Anyone that wanted to hunt
got a chance, including a few of the Gypsies. It was a
grand time for everyone.

Except it was not so grand for Samuel, who was
excluded from the hunting due to his injury. That fact
aggravated his mind far more than the wound pained his
arm. He spent a couple of days sulking about it before
he decided to do something about it. He consulted the
Gypsy Queen, who re-wrapped the injured arm in such a
way that it was almost straight instead of bent for a
sling. That evening, when it was dark, he tried his bow

and found he could draw it with a tolerable degree of pain.

In the morning, Samuel met the prince as he was making ready for the morning hunt. "I'm ready to go collect on our hunt now," Samuel whispered.

Prince Lohman was puzzled as he stated, "You can't draw your bow."

"Maybe I have some Gypsy magic up my sleeve," Samuel retorted. "I just wish Levi was well enough to troop along with us. He has seemed down."

As it turned out, Samuel could only draw his bow a few times before the pain was too great. But his spirits lifted considerably from the hunt, despite the good-natured razing from the prince who had to finish Samuel's second boar.

That day turned out to be the turning point for Levi as well. When he learned that Samuel had been hunting and had scored two boars, hope returned to Levi's heart, and where hope grows, despair recedes. The sense of life as usual was returning around him, and his pain level had settled to something manageable. It also did not hurt his feelings that Gretta spent an inordinate amount of time helping him with his daily chores. He found her company quite pleasurable.

It was clear to everyone that a romance was blossoming between Levi and Gretta. But the disabled Gypsy could not see his way around the one giant obstacle: He had lost his ability to ply his trade. That concerned him, but did not stop them, and in due time that would prove to be not as big an obstacle as he had expected.

On the last day of the Jamboree, the king came to Levi along with Queen Sarah, Lord William, Lady Sylvia, Prince Lohman, Princess Katrina, Elise, and even Gavin. Levi was more than a little flustered by the gathering of important people. The Gypsy jumped to his feet and began to bow, but the king immediately put him at ease. "Please, Levi, your tremendous sacrifice for the safety of my daughter was monumental. You are forthwith instructed to sit as if you are part of the family any time you are in our presence."

Everyone beamed with great smiles, and Levi blushed self-consciously as he sat back down. It was obvious that the royal family had discussed the meeting in advance.

The king caveated his statement with, "Obviously, there will be times in court when it is appropriate for all present to rise and ..."

Sarah rolled her eyes as she interjected, "Oh, Lawrence, this isn't the time for those kinds of instructions. He'll pick that stuff up in due time."

Then there came the awkward silence that happens when everyone is unsure of what to say next. Out of the blue, Levi picked up the conversation with a humorous quip. "Well, Your Highness, I would have trimmed my beard. I normally do so every ten days, but I seem to lose count at nine these days!"

The ice was suddenly broken, and everyone burst into laughter. Levi made a few more humorous quips, and the laughter came faster. In those few moments, Levi essentially came back to life. He stopped short when he almost said he would grab his juggling clubs. Involuntarily he glanced at Katrina. Her look of empathy was mixed with something he could not identify.

King Lawrence cleared his throat and made his statement. "Levi, I would like to offer you a position as the chief entertainer at the castle in Falcon's Crest. I realize you will have a healing time before you would be able to resume all of your tricks. It will require that you give up the Gypsy life, but there will be numerous travel opportunities each year."

Levi sat, mouth agape with surprise. When he finally regained his faculties, he glanced around to share the news with Gretta. But Gretta was on duty somewhere.

The king nodded as he explained, "She already knows. That's why I had her on duty, so she wouldn't spill the news before I could make the formal offer."

With his thoughts spinning rapidly, Levi asked, "What shall I do with my cart and donkey?"

"You know, it just occurred to me that your cart will come in quite handy some day. We've plenty of space to keep it at the castle," the king replied.

*　　*　　*　　*　　*

When Gretta found Levi later that afternoon, she seemed distant, which confused the Gypsy. "Master Levi, you've got a position of authority at the castle now," Gretta stoically stated. Her smile was genuine, but her heart was clearly troubled.

"I don't think it's an important position," Levi replied. His confusion was also evident.

"The king says your official title is Master Levi, Steward of Entertainment," she countered with stern-faced formality. "In my position, I'm to refer to you as Master Levi."

"Must you use that title when we are not in public?" Levi asked.

"I must use that title any time you require it of me," she replied.

"Then the only time I require it is when the king would consider it necessary for formalities," Levi thoughtfully responded.

Gretta's face lit up with her grin as she ordered, "Let's get that hand of yours dressed and wrapped back up. That Gypsy Queen is one sharp lady. No one heals like this when the leeches work on them in the castle. In fact, often as not, they get worse."

"We tend to shy away from their ilk, as a general rule," Levi rejoined. He was very aware of her proximity as she gently applied the salve to his wounded hand.

Levi tried to think of a tactful approach to the subject of courting. His mental search proved fruitless, so he blurted, "How do your people signify if they are available to be courted?"

Homeward Bound

The Gypsy Jamboree was dismissed in the usual manner. The parting blessing was repeated as each cart rolled out onto the road. Last minute arrangements were shouted as the general disorder degenerated into near chaos. As far as partings went, that one was as near normal as it had ever been.

The king's party was divided into two groups. The first was the carts and their accompanying servants. Those would naturally take the road back to Falcon's Crest. The second group started as a near mutiny when Sarah and Sylvia discovered they were not going to see the citadel ruins. It was not that King Lawrence was trying to keep anyone from it, he simply did not realize how strong the draw was for his wife and sister-in-law to see the place of such legend.

When all the emotional talking had been calmed, the king agreed to take a company of soldiers and show his wife and her sister the old ruin. He asked for volunteers from his guard unit, but he had not anticipated that every single one of them would instantly volunteer to be in that party. It would have proven to be a logistical mess had everyone else not wanted to go as well. In the end, it was a handful of crestfallen servants that had to accompany the service carts who missed out.

The king's party wound their way through the forest trail that morning in a barely perceptible drizzle. The sun was shielded by thick clouds that hung close to the earth, creating a surreal mist through which the long line of riders quietly plodded.

For Sylvia, there was an intense sense of anticipation. In the shadow of that type of expectation resides the lurking sense of eminent disappointment. As she pondered her thoughts and attempted to sort the feelings from the facts, Sarah rode up beside her. They rode along in silence for a time before Sarah asked, "Are we about to suffer our lifetime's greatest disillusion?"

Sylvia realized that she and her sister were having similar thoughts about the legendary citadel. Before her logical mind could intervene, she replied, "No."

Sarah did not ask any further questions, but also did not offer any thoughts either.

The group began to enter the clearing that had been trampled down by the previous week's activity. The charred marking at the door made the citadel more visible than it should have been. Lord William was leading the procession and got a slight whiff of wood smoke. Captain Cornelius, who was beside him, smelled it at the same time. They made eye contact and William whispered, "Someone's inside."

Without warning, the captain called out a command, and the royal guard launched into action. The royal family and their guests were immediately encircled by a dozen soldiers who all held drawn weapons. Another dozen made a rear battle line facing the direction they had come. Their lances were in the attack ready position by the time the line formed. And the remaining two dozen guards formed a double curved front battle line. The soldiers in the front line each held his lance at the ready. The second line of soldiers, which was aligned between the lancers, one horse's length behind, each held his sword at the attack ready position.

All of the maneuvers were executed within a few heartbeats and William, who was accustomed to working in silence and stealth, was duly impressed. As he wondered what his role should be, he realized, with some surprise, that he had strung his bow and he held an arrow on the string.

There was a tense few minutes as the captains discussed the next move. As lifelong soldiers, their lives had been spent training for such events. But the absence of an adversary baffled them. William rode up to join their conference in time to hear Captain Roen say, "How do we battle against a cave stronghold with a tiny door?"

Captain Cornelius excitedly replied, "First order is to keep the royal family safe above all. We should leave and return with an expeditionary party to rout the remainder of that gang of thugs!"

"Yes, but this may be our best opportunity to completely annihilate them!" Captain Roen protested.

Lord William interjected, "Leave me with your six best close-quarter fighters and, when you have the others a safe distance away, we'll go in and engage them."

"I'm going in with you!" The three men turned even though they knew instantly who had spoken.

William rolled his eyes as he retorted, "This really is a matter for trained soldiers, honey. You should get back inside the barrier of guards."

She gave him a look that indicated her disdain for his idea. "Da, they couldn't even stop me from slipping out."

Both captains looked back at their soldiers with some degree of agitation. One of the sergeants gave an exasperated shrug of the shoulders.

"See, now you've gotten diligent soldiers in trouble!" William exclaimed.

Elise sighed heavily, then urged, "Come on, Da, we can ride down there as fast as these horses will run. We'll jump through that doorway, you go right, I'll go left, and we stick arrows into anyone who doesn't surrender. It'll be over before this whole army thing can get started!"

William knew the plan was ridiculous even though that was exactly what he wanted to do. As he opened his mouth to reclaim some degree of sanity, a shout went up from the troop. William spun toward the citadel and drew as he did so. Everyone froze as Father Geoffrey led a solitary figure out of the citadel. The man with the priest held his hands high in surrender, and the two captains rode quickly to meet the pair. William and Elise rode down behind them.

The tension had been high, and Captain Cornelius exploded, "What is the meaning of this?"

Suddenly he recognized the thin man. His eyes were less puffy and the red was gone, but he was still rather pathetic looking. "You again! Are you in cahoots with this gang?" the captain demanded.

Before the man could answer, the captain turned to the priest, "Father? What were you thinking? This could have been dangerous!"

The priest, who was notorious for holding his silence, held up his hands to calm the agitated soldier. "Brother Cornelius, I have read committals over four dozen men on this outing. It is high time the bloodshed cease if it can possibly be averted. I just walked into the cave and asked this man what he was doing here."

The king came charging down and, before his horse came to a stop, he demanded, "What is he doing here?"

The startled man dropped to a knee in a bow, "My Lord, I was making a shelter for the winter. And some boxes for my bees."

Everyone was surprised, except the priest of course. King Lawrence asked, "You keep bees?"

"I used to, long ago," the man replied.

Looking around for any sign of the insects, the king again asked, "Where are your bees?"

"Oh, they're still in their tree, Sire. I need to finish the boxes before I can transfer the colonies," the man answered simply.

"And you're setting up a place to live in this cave?" The king's tone had softened a bit.

Hesitantly the man responded, "I was ... if that is permissible."

The little man looked from the king to Lord William to the captains to Elise, then back to the king. Everyone was pondering him. He glanced at the priest for reassurance. No one blinked.

Finally the king stated, "I had considered what to do with this place. It could be a strategic military outpost in the Barrens. But it would still be a hidden secret were it not for my wife and her sister. Your residence here may be temporary, so do not get too comfortable." He paused, then inquired, "Do you have somewhere else to live?"

The dejected little man shook his head to the negative. "Do you have a name?" the king asked.

The man thought for a moment to remember. He had been the village drunk for over a decade, and had no significant dealings with anyone during that time. "Your Majesty, I was Simeon the Bee Keeper, before my wife died. I took to drink to stop the sorrow and ... and I guess I never stopped drinking." After a brief pause he added, "I think I would like to be Simeon again."

King Lawrence motioned for the rest of the party to join them as he responded, "Simeon the Bee Keeper. You do well, and when this place is assigned to a purpose, I will warrant you shall have somewhere to go."

The little man bowed, and when he stood, his face beamed with tears and a smile. The priest gave him an avuncular pat on the shoulder.

As soon as the captains had evaluated the cave and secured two soldiers at the back entrance, the queen and her sister entered the hall. Others followed. When their eyes adjusted to the gloomy light, they marveled at everything. The bell was just as it had been described in old writings, and Katrina pointed out the significant places and retold the events that had transpired there, while some of the people milled about in fascination.

"*Enter to find refuge, Enter to find peace,*" the priest mused. "This place may have been a monastery."

Sylvia corrected him, "No, Father, it was a military stronghold. In ancient times, the neighboring king would send troops to the aid of those who took refuge here."

The priest stood silently without breaking eye contact with Sylvia. Finally she asked, "Is there more?"

The priest wiped the soot from the cave wall beside of the doorway and replied. "The twenty-third Psalm is engraved next to the opening."

Everyone gathered close and it was clear for all to see. Those who could read Latin were duly impressed.

"Should this place be restored as a monastery?" Prince Lohman asked solemnly.

Before the king could respond, Captain Roen interjected, "Your Majesty, this is the strategically perfect place to set up a military outpost to secure these wild lands. Your father spoke often of doing such a thing."

William spoke up and added, "What about the bee keeper?"

The king entered into a brief conversation with both captains about the feasibility and strategic location for an outpost. The supply roads and raw materials that could be returned from the mountains factored heavily into their excited conversation. They had discovered several smaller halls off of the main hall that had been hidden by old dead foliage prior to the fire. The possibilities began to escalate in their conversation.

Ominously, the doorway shadowed. Gretta entered cautiously, almost coaxing Levi into the great hall of the citadel. A hush fell over everyone in the cave.

Levi had opted to not go into the place when everyone else went in. His mind had painted it full of nightmarish memories that he could not cope with. Gretta, though she was a maid, was a wise woman. She was also committed to Levi's total healing, which included his mind. She knew he needed to confront the seat of his terrors to conquer them.

Once Levi was inside the cave, he stood with his heart pounding so loudly in his ears, he did not hear the silence of the others. All eyes followed the Gypsy. When he spied the column that had held him and the princess in their shackle, he was visibly shaken.

Mustering his courage, Levi walked directly to the stone beam. With Gretta at his side, he gingerly put his hand into the hole. Katrina slipped up beside him and put her arm around his shoulders, as he examined the fateful structure. "There is still no explanation for this carved hole," he heard his voice calmly state.

The princess, through free-flowing tears, whispered, "This is the place you forever changed from Levi the hapless Entertainer, to Levi the selfless Hero."

Sometimes, healing takes place in a moment. Levi relaxed and, stepping back from the column, asked, "Where's the bell?"

Katrina reverently showed Levi the stairs and bell and pointed out the bronze mallet. She asked, "Would you like to hear it?"

"Oh, no! There is no danger now. And I already heard it. I knew you would be saved when I heard it," he replied softly.

Gretta nodded and she added, "I thought he was taking a turn for the worse. He couldn't sleep more than a few minutes at a time. But when that bell rang, he sat straight up out of his delirium and said to me, 'The princess is saved!' He said, 'The king will find her now.' Then he passed right out asleep like a baby."

Levi turned red and replied, "I don't remember saying anything, I just remember hearing the bell."

Looking around with a new sense of awe, Levi asked no one in particular, "What's to be done with this place? It has amazing sound."

Then before anyone could respond to his question, he began to sing *The Death Ride of Bogaaz*.

The ancient tale of Prince Bogaaz and his faithful few warriors facing the overwhelming armies of Shalman was woven masterfully into music. The doleful song wafted eerily throughout the great hall. And as the last notes about the hopeless battle echoed into silence, everyone stood speechlessly still for a long moment.

Finally, King Lawrence breathlessly exclaimed, "Where did you come up with that song? It made the hair on my neck hackle!"

Levi was somewhat abashed and stuttered, "I, um, it's, an, um, an ancient Persian tale, and I just made up the tune just now."

The king shook his head slowly as he muttered, "And they call court jesters, fools. That was anything but foolish." He paused, then added with a glance around, "That was your second show-stopping performance in this place." He looked at Levi with a fresh eye and asked, "What do you think would be a good use of this place?"

Levi looked around again and shrugged. "I don't really know. It was lost for so long, then it became a refuge for evil. It seems to me like it should be redeemed as a place of good. A place for people to come to for healing and restoration. A gathering place for the dearest and closest of friends. It's too bad there are no people to inhabit it ..."

Levi stopped abruptly and apologized, "But, I'm sorry Sire, I've been rambling on."

As everyone else watched in anticipation, the king patted Levi's shoulder and declared, "You, my friend, are visionary."

The End

Post Scripts

Not Unnerved

Elise's senses tingled deep within her being. She rolled out of her blankets and quickly got dressed. Nothing had happened that she could tell, but she did not want to miss it. As she slipped silently from her tent, she noted the sentries by their fires. She looked around carefully, peering into the shadows between the posts. Everything seemed to be still. So she waited.

It was just a matter of minutes before she caught the faintest hint of motion. It was by the tent of her parents. She realized that her father had set his tent up strategically so that the flap would be in the shadow of the watch fires. *Clever,* she thought, *I'll have to remember that trick next time.* She watched for any sign of movement. *He's spotted my silhouette,* she thought. Ever so gently, she raised her quiver. The fletchings of the arrows were the traditional woodsman's signal. William responded in kind and moved toward her as he slipped his quiver on his back.

They met halfway and, in a barely audible whisper, she said, "Boars?"

"Hmm, I'm thinking five," was his hushed reply.

"Do we slip out silently?" Elise whispered.

"Na. The king's boys have been stressed enough. I don't want to unnerve them any further," he breathed.

Silently, they approached the sentry that stood guard closest to the desired trail into the woods. William gently tapped on the man's shoulder.

"GAA!" the man all but shrieked as he whirled. His sword was half-drawn when he recognized Lord William. "Good heavens! You scared half the life out of me!" he stage whispered. The man was visibly shaking.

"That was his interpretation of not unnerving you," Elise remarked with a grin.

Upon realizing he was in the presence of an attractive young lady, the man managed to regain his composure. "Will you be heading out of camp, M' Lord?" he asked, as if there were other options.

"Yes, Elise and I will be hunting in the red marsh," William replied. "Would you please request that the king send ten strong men, at midmorning, with some rope?"

"Yes, sir," the guard replied. He was obviously having trouble keeping his eyes off Elise.

As they turned toward the woods, William, in just a loud enough voice for the man to hear, said, "I'll bet you a silver schilling, I arrow two at a time before you do!"

Elise, oblivious to the game her father was playing on the young guard's mind, replied playfully, "Oh, so you're throwing away money now. Well, I'll be happy to take it from you."

When William and Elise had slipped comfortably away from the camp, William held up his hand to signal a stop. They stood a moment and Elise whispered, "What?"

"We're waiting for Gavin," William whispered his reply.

"Why?" Elise was confused.

"Because he slipped out of the camp while we were speaking with the guard," William sighed with resignation.

"Can I frighten him?" Elise's whispered question contained far too much anticipation.

"No," her father whispered back. The word from his lips carried no emotion, but his tone projected an impish grin.

*   *   *   *   *

At the morning muster of the royal guard, just as the night watch reports were about to be called out, Lady Sylvia tapped Captain Cornelius on the shoulder.

"Captain, have your men seen Lord William, or Elise, or Gavin, my little guy, this morning?"

Partly in exasperation, and partly in jest, the captain turned toward his men and exclaimed, "Is anyone left in this camp bedsides us?"

Milk and Honey

It was six years to the day after Levi cut off his thumb, that the bell was rung for the second time. It had been rededicated as the King's Salute, and announced the arrival of the royal party to Levi's Refuge. The ancient citadel's restoration had been completed, and the Gypsy Jamboree had, by the king's invitation, migrated to it.

The amenities were considerably better than most villages, because the small community had been planned carefully to be self-sustaining as well as resource producing. Their primary product was lumber, but there was a substantial business of honey and dairy products as well.

After all the formalities had been tended to by the king at the kingdom's most remote outpost, the royal party and the Gypsies were able to begin their celebration. Their happy reunion was dampened somewhat by the sad news of the passing of the Gypsy Queen. The king offered his deep regrets. And the details were shared that she had surpassed the age of one hundred by a good many years. It was widely believed by the Gypsies that she had held on to life until she was satisfied that the citadel was properly restored.

Day two of the Jamboree began with Lord William instructing some Gypsy children how to shoot a bow. Most of the adults turned out to watch the event, because it was expected to be highly amusing.

Levi and his family were enjoying the second day of the best Jamboree he could remember when a page rushed up to him and whispered, "Master Levi, come quickly! I fear Princess Katrina has seen a ghost!"

The page raced off to summon Elise with the same message, and Levi and Gretta rushed from the game field. As they hastened to the refuge, Levi's mind revisited dark memories of the place.

Princess Katrina met them at the main door and jabbered incomprehensibly all the way through the Great Hall to the back chamber in a storage room.

Finally she stopped and pointed at a slim young woman. Everyone stared at the girl.

She would not have been considered a particularly pretty girl, but for her radiant smile. "This is Isabel. She's a goatherd. *The* goatherd here. Her uncle is the bee keeper." Katrina paused for everyone to catch up. "Her father was the innkeeper that was killed by that wretched woman outlaw ..."

Gretta immediately embraced the young woman in a smothering hug. Levi stood awkwardly watching his wife console the girl as if the incident had been the day prior.

Katrina continued her story, "She is also to be married to Sergeant Eric, who was nearly killed the same way." She paused for everyone to take in the drama of the connections. "I was conversing with Isabel, and she told me her quarters, until next week when she gets married, of course. Anyway, her quarters are downstairs with the Sisters and other unmarried women on staff." Again the princess dramatically paused, obviously expecting a response. She repeated, "Downstairs."

Levi crinkled his brow and replied, "There is no downstairs ..." His words trailed off into uncertainty.

Katrina backed a few paces further into the supply room, beckoning them as she did. It took Levi a few moments to register what his eyes were seeing. A round planked wooden door was held open by a stout rope. It was fastened to a stone column through a carved hole. Upon recognition, Levi caught his breath with a gasp. He looked at the stairs that had been hewn from the stone slope that led down to a chamber below. His head jerked up and he whispered, "How did the wooden door not burn? How did it survive all those years of decay?"

A beaming Katrina answered, "This is a replacement. The great round stone table in the dining hall was the original door. Simeon and Isabel found it when they were cleaning out the old cave. This cave."

Isabel interjected, "Uncle and I never could budge it until the king's men came, and it took a good many of them to move it."

"Why would someone go to such efforts to cover a chamber with an immovable stone?" Levi wondered aloud.

"Oh," Isabel volunteered, "The cave leads out to several other openings."

"To keep out raiders. And the opening below is too narrow for more than one man at a a time to reach the door," Levi speculated. "It's brilliant."

After some further discussion, Levi and Gretta wandered back out to rejoin the Gypsy events. Elise asked, "Is it permissible for us to look around downstairs?"

"Yes, of course," Isabel replied.

As Elise and Katrina looked curiously about the lower chamber, Katrina mused aloud, "This place fills me with wonder. What other mysteries does this place hold?"

The End ...